THE LEFT TURN

Two Lives, Worlds Apart

BOOK 1 IN THE SPLIT UNIVERSE SERIES

Becky Parker Geist

Edited by David Colin Carr
Cover art by Milli Jane
Cover design by Suzanne Parrott
Interior design by John Byrne Barry

DEDICATION

To my daughters, Elise, Jes and Jerrilee—
my best friends

"As Harvard professor emeritus of English, John Paul Eakin, points out, memory of the narrative of our lives is 'not only literally essential to the continuation of identity, but also crucial in the sense that it is constantly revising and editing the remembered past to square with the needs and requirements of the self we have become in any present.'"

—Carl Buchheit, Ph.D., Ellie Schamber, Ph.D.

"We live in forgetfulness. But always there is the opportunity to live our life fully. When we drink water, we can be aware that we are drinking water. When we walk, we can be aware that we are walking. Mindfulness is available to us in every moment."

—Thich Nhat Hanh

"There are no two people with the same reality."

—Carl Buchheit, Ph.D.

Prologue

I turned left. Just leaned slightly. Without thought.

My calf muscles screaming GO . . . GO . . . GO . . . GO!

I pumped hard. Desperately. A hill of fear rising in front of me. I pushed harder. My heart pounded furiously.

The air: dense, thick. Its salt sliced at my cheeks. The street was level, but my breathing strained and erratic. GO! The asphalt blurred—black and gray and white.

Colorful cars smeared past in short streaks of finger paint: periwinkle, cherry, azure, burgundy. Yellow flashed on the left: a cab. A sage green vehicle sped by me, then slowed and stopped. I looked up. My legs obeyed the red octagonal sign, my hands squeezed the brakes, but my mind sailed through without slowing. My legs asked the question my mind could not slow enough to formulate: what did I just do?

A sound—like glass shattering—snapped the question in two as I pedaled forward through the intersection. The question "forward toward what?" never formed, all thought gone. Yet a feeling like a growing shadow remained. One thing was certain: there was no going back.

CHAPTER ONE

The Left Turn

I've lived on the edge of anxiety always, but no pills for me. Mom's soul crumpled under their influence. It was heartbreaking and ironic: she was unable to discern what was happening—because of what was happening.

I wanted some natural way to handle stress. Started reading books on meditation. Supposedly a life-changing experience. But I still don't get it. There's got to be more to it than just sitting and breathing. I'm better at moving and breathing. Once we get settled maybe I'll find a class or group—there are plenty of options here in the Bay Area. Maybe in a couple weeks.

I turned forty-six this year and I feel like I'm getting stronger. Not older. Good, because biking the hills around here is going to take some serious muscle. So many of the people I know—not that I have many friends, because I don't, and none out here in California—are slowing down, putting on weight, complaining about how hard it is to stay on a diet, or how they have no time to exercise, it's expensive to keep buying clothes to keep up with weight changes. Et cetera! The people I left behind in the Midwest spent an exhausting amount of time in that conversation.

Just this morning—even before James was up—I was scrolling through my social media and got fed up with some long, ridiculous conversation about a cabbage soup diet. I hope they enjoy breaking wind together to battle the bulge—I won't notice, I'm half a continent way now. I deleted my Facebook profile, vowing not to return. It was like a hit of espresso. I logged in to Instagram.

"Can't you do anything in moderation? What are you trying to prove?" I swatted the air as if my dead mother's voice were a mosquito buzzing my ear. Rebellion revved, GET ME OUT OF HERE! I performed a mass exodus from all social media, deleted every profile. Almost delirious, I deleted my synced accounts, then all the contacts in my phone. Then my laptop, without even looking at them first. "ARE YOU SURE?" It wanted confirmation this was no accident. And, no, I wasn't sure. I was manic. This felt as good as binging on homemade cookies. I almost wished for another stack of accounts to obliterate. My publisher would probably kill me for it, but I was beyond considering undoing the undoing of my life—so ready to purge.

After my fervor cooled, I made tea in the sole unbroken smokey-blue mug from the set James and I bought for our first apartment. I was relishing the feeling of freedom from people, their problems, our history—the overwhelming input from the external world that had been progressively clogging my overloaded neurons. Time for a new outlook. Maybe our move is about to provide that.

I took my cup out to the small porch. It was sunny, a perfect sixty-five degrees. James was bouncing on his toes on the front step, looking restless as always, sipping coffee between bounces. I looked away. Maybe the move would also dispel the dark cloud that hung over me when he was around. Hope for change scented the air between us. That thought sparked an idea for the protagonist coming to life in my novel.

"Come on, Hannah, let's ride."

I stared blankly at the oversized driveway, wondering if I would regret any of the deleting. Almost certainly. It must be possible to live without the barrage. There are many people in the world functioning adequately without it. Had been for centuries. Devices breaking, getting lost or stolen all the time. Websites get hacked and shut down. Wi-fi hardly reliable. No one is dying from computer viruses or shortness of data or congestive data failure. I'd gotten bloated from overconsumption, strained with communication exertion. The aftermath might even produce good material for an article or short story.

"It's a fucking gorgeous day!" James exclaimed.

"Your expletive doesn't fit your adjective," I replied.

"Shaking your vocabulary bootie in my direction is not going to distract me."

"I'm not. . ." Well, maybe I was. It wasn't that I didn't want to go biking. I was itching to. Truth is, I've a lifetime habit of depriving myself of things I enjoy. As if I don't deserve to do fun stuff. "Do something useful." That wasn't Mom's voice, but just as familiar.

"I need to unpack, get organized," I protested. But maybe a ride would enhance the exhilaration of all that deleting.

"It'll start raining any day and keep going for months. That's what the locals say. You can hold off unpacking and all that crap 'til the first rainy day. Half our stuff is MIA anyway."

"True . . ."

Like a hound picking up a scent, James looked me straight in the eyes. But my mind had taken a detour, just like our stuff. Somehow the movers had managed to lose the boxes I had so meticulously packed and very clearly labeled. So far, all the boxes appeared to be James's. I was pissed. How could all our boxes be packed into one truck in Illinois and yet not all arrive together in California? Last week, when they delivered the first installment, the feckless driver of the truck explained there'd been a short layover while that truck was unloaded, then everything reloaded into a different truck headed for the Bay Area the next day. The conversation replayed in my mind . . .

"Sorry, Mrs. Wescott—"

"I am not Mrs. Wescott."

"Sorry, I shouldn't have assumed—"

"Agreed, you should not have presumed. But your inaccurate and, frankly, discourteous assumption is irrelevant to the more pressing and pertinent question regarding the current whereabouts of the segment of our belongings that bear the magenta labels. Could you elucidate that point—preferably without further platitudinous ingratiation?" I bored a well-deserved glare first at the driver, then at his partner. They wore matching gray coveralls, the driver's way too big, and his husky coworker's rather too small. I wanted to send them to the bathroom to swap uniforms. My eyes dropped to the red and white

4

embroidered logo "Interstate Movers: Moving You to Any State."

"Your motto would be more accurate as: 'Moving You to the State of Aggravation.'"

James, behind me, stifled a snicker. Which fueled my ire. The moving guys looked at each other, shrugged, and spoke at the same time, with opposite responses—neither of which was an actual answer.

"No."

"Yeah."

The driver looked at James, gave a wobbly half smile, and, reaching around me cautiously, handed him the clipboard with the papers for him to sign off.

I tried to intercept it. "What are you doing? Don't sign that!" James swept it out of my reach. I grabbed at it again, but he dodged deftly. "If you sign that, we'll never see the rest of our boxes again!"

James took the pen from the man whose buttons pulled dangerously against his buttonholes, noted that several boxes were missing and signed his name. He handed the clipboard back to the driver. When the guy reached for the pen, James withdrew it dramatically. He put his arm around me protectively and said with feigned solidarity. "Don't you worry, baby. We're going to hold this pen as collateral until we get our boxes with the red labels—"

"Magenta."

"As I said, magenta labels. Magenta. Make a note." He jabbed the air with the pen at the movers to emphasize the color. The driver looked at the pen in James's hand. "Not with this pen. No. Don't expect to see this slate gray pen with raspberry cream letters again, not until those boxes are delivered. You got that?"

The men in gray looked uncertain. "We'll notify the office," the driver mumbled, and left us on the front steps.

"Consider this a housewarming gift." James smiled, handing me the pen. He walked inside. I fumed in the cooling breeze.

Now here we were, five days later, and no boxes richer. On the porch with James again trying to get me to let go, to smile. All that had arrived for me was my bike, laptop, and the carry-on toiletries and spare underwear I'd brought on the plane.

"Come on. You need this as much as I do," James cajoled.

"Ruby needs a tune-up." Twice already I'd lost the chain in quick downshifts on my trek up the steep hill to the new rental, but I hadn't found a bike shop yet.

"Why did you ask for a house with a view when you know I rely on my bike to get around?" A reflection of who was at the center of his orbit.

He looked amused. "Great way to build muscle. Don't be such a stick-in-the-mud."

"I'm not!"

"I could go without you . . ."

He knew that would feel worse.

"I guess a ride would give me a feel for the area. Maybe we'll pass a thrift store, and I can get something else to wear until the magenta boxes arrive." I sighed dramatically.

James bounced up and kissed the top of my head, nearly knocking over my tea. His bushy beard caught strands of my hair that rose with static. "I already topped up the tires with air. We're good to go. Fill up your water bottle, and I'll grab us some snacks. Oh, and I mapped out a route across the Golden Gate Bridge—which should be fucking awesome—and lots of other places. Gonna be great."

"I have to wax my chain first."

"Have it your way." He was already halfway inside, happily bustling about in the kitchen. When we had met—at barely eighteen—his easy, youthful happiness was what I'd fallen for. He showed me how to have fun, to laugh—there had been so little growing up with Dad angry most of the time and Mom in a daze. James had crawled into my heart and flicked the happiness switch. I remembered that I had experienced that feeling of lightness, but that light went out again with the avalanche of my world crumbling on my birthday. Twenty-eight years is a long time to search for another light switch. But here we are, still at it.

Wishing I felt as happy as he looked, I turned toward the garage. Have it my way? I never have things my way!

In the nearly empty two-car garage, I grabbed the new bottle of chain wax. The shape of it reminded me of a child-size Elmer's glue.

James was whistling. I grumbled.

Mom "tsked" from the director's chair between my ears. "Stop whining and think about someone else for a change." She was right, though I hated the fact that she'd taken up residence there. Rent free. Even though James rarely let on, his happiness could be fragile. How could I begrudge him any happiness after what had happened four years ago? But just when life hit him hard, I landed a book deal I'd worked so hard to get—a dream come true! The happiness that had finally broken through for me had withered. It never had a chance. Celebration was inappropriate. Happiness crouched in the shadow of tragedy. A mockery.

The garage door rumbled closed while I headed back to the house. It was littered with boxes—all James's. Being stuff-less was weird, almost as freeing as it was annoying. My one set of clothes, however, was losing its appeal. In the balance between shopping or researching ancient grains for the next book in my "Killer Menu" mystery series—shopping loses. Every time.

I grabbed my daypack and found James in the kitchen. "Okay, almost ready." I gulped a glass of water.

"Got your phone?" James asked as he stuffed his into his pocket.

"Not bringing it—need a jail break from my cell."

James looked at me sideways. Something was different—I think we both felt it. He pulled me into a hug and kissed me. His beard tickled. His hug lingered and tightened—passion or pain? I couldn't tell. Maybe just my imagination, but warmth started to rise—a glimmer. I tried to hold onto it, tightening my grip. He responded in kind. It felt like a goodbye hug, with a capital G. That scared me. I pulled back.

His eyes twinkled—he hadn't noticed. "Great idea! I love it. I'll leave mine behind, too. If we get lost, we'll just have to suck it up and talk to strangers." He winked. Easy for him—he's great with people, but I hadn't yet memorized our new address. He went back to filling snack bags with nuts and dried fruit.

My eyes lingered on him—the pressure of tears mounting. Hijacking them before they did me, I grabbed my thin jacket out of the hall closet, then dashed downstairs for a final bathroom stop.

Riding and writing have always been my life, my Houdini hacks, my escapes. Whether someone else's or my own, the written word opens doors I can casually step through and vanish into other worlds. A novel covers only a prime-time slice of the characters' lives, but great authors always leave me longing to keep living with the characters in their worlds, dealing with their problems, charmed by their eloquence or brilliantly crafted stammering.

Even long novels always end too soon for me. The characters' lives might become less exciting after the climax—but as long as they avoid mundane conversations about cabbage soup and prescriptions and illness competitions, they're bound to be better than social media.

From the dresser I picked up my most recent literary find: Where Flows the Creek: A Romp in the eDimension by David Colin Carr about an elf adventuring among creatures of the natural world. Enticing and magical. I was about twenty pages into it and if James deigned to take a breather at any point on our ride, I might get to read further.

Last week, the day after the "moving experience" with Interstate Mutt and Jeff, we took a bus into the city to explore—including a visit to the Asian Art Museum. I'd taken a book that day as well, but it felt rude to read in that archive of others' lives. James had been testy at breakfast, so I trod carefully. I don't really get Asian art, which makes me feel culturally inadequate. When museum displays don't speak to me, I have little to say about them. But I knew he'd take my lack of interest personally. So, I had tried to participate with enthusiasm.

I decided to leave the book behind and went upstairs. From about age eight, when I'd become a fluent, high consumption reader, my mother complained endlessly that I was avoiding life, not dealing with the real world. I'd heard "You're missing out" so many times by the time I was eleven, I'd stopped even looking up. "On what?"

"On things like making friends and—"

At which point I'd squint up at her with a "Seriously?" look.

"—and, well, real things." Her mind stalled.

I couldn't deny it, not if I were honest—which I tried not to be with my parents. Too hazardous. Their "real world" was not conducive to real experiences—at least not any that interested me. But the worlds shaped by ink and paper drew me in, surrounding me with vivid sensations and fascinating people. Worlds with feelings: love and tragedy and fear and joy. The tang of saltwater on an ocean mist and the muscles of a wild mustang as I ride through the lush field of a land no one could find in geography books. Those feelings were how I knew that I existed.

Outside, James loaded up the bikes onto the rental car and we headed out to the parking lot on the north side of the Golden Gate Bridge. The lot was full.

"Damn it," James grumbled. "We should've left earlier."

Feeling blamed, I twisted around to look for options.

James lurched us out of the lot. Finding a spot downhill on the other side of the highway, we climbed out and unloaded. "Lot of uphill to get to the bridge." He was irritated, but I could tell he was trying not to show it.

"Better starting than ending uphill," I offered.

He sighed, shifted his demeanor, and gave me a smile. "True that. Ready?"

I envied his ability to let go like that.

Saturday and the weather was perfect: clear blue sky, cool, no wind.

The bridge was loud with traffic noise rebounding between the I-beams and railings, but the view of the ocean and bay, the cliffs of the headlands, neighborhood beaches in the city, sailboats and ferries and freighters and tugs, gulls and seals frolicking—it was enough to make you want time to stand still.

James raced ahead across the bridge, assuming I was right behind him. He lived as if he was always late. For what? An appointment with death? I followed, but at the first tower, I stopped. The traffic noise almost disappeared behind the massive stanchion. A glorious moment of refuge. Below, a kayaker paddled near the Marin shore, cutting through white caps—there and gone, seconds ticking by without distinction. I reflected how everything can change in an instant. Might he capsize and drown with land so near?

I have a terror of drowning, of not being able to breathe.

Watching the turbulent salt water, tears welled. A sudden rush of oxygen caught in my throat—panic right on its heels.

James reappeared suddenly, startling me, kicking the panic up a gear. His thick, dark brown hair hung over his forehead, damp with sweat. "Problem with the bike?" Unvoiced: some reason you're not keeping up? I heard it anyway, teasing my fear of drowning. But he was smiling—happy to be racing along, getting to the other side of the next whatever. I felt like I was being dragged along by a leash.

I appreciated the thought, at least in theory. But part of me wished he'd forgotten me—let me slip from his mind so I could commune with the seals and the kayaker, find solace in their ease, their playfulness.

"Ready?"

I nodded, swallowing grief for the few deep breaths that might have been. It was easier to smile and ride on. Easier to drown slowly.

Passing the second span of the bridge, we sped down long curving hills, the ocean on our right, towards the Palace of the Legion of Honor. We entered the main hall with the Rodin sculptures. I was captivated. "They make me want to cry."

"Why, what's wrong?"

"Nothing's wrong—everything is . . . is right. I mean the story is right here in their faces, their sacrifice." James clearly didn't know the history. "In the Hundred Years' War, England's Edward III laid siege to Calais. The people were starving. The only way to save the city was for six of the city's leaders to walk out with nooses around their necks, carrying the keys to the city, expecting to be executed. Their expressions, the—the fierce determination to save their city no matter the personal cost. Defeat, but also pride because they'd each volunteered to be one of the six."

"Rodin's amazing, but also part of their permanent collection. Let's check out the wearable art—it's the last day for that show. Shall we?"

I tore my eyes away from the burghers and followed James down the broad marble stairs, unfocused. The first couple of rooms contained pieces we both appreciated, and our conversation relaxed. James moved steadily on. In the third room near the back wall was a small, elaborate mask that reeled me in. Created out of words clipped from newspapers and magazines, it asked, "is the mAsk on me or aM i In the mask?" and "can you LoOk inSide?" and "can'T yOu see me?" and "can they ReAlly REad Us?"

It ensnared me—questions inside questions through selective capitalization, so subtle. The deeper query: "AM I LOST OR ARE U?" The layers of questions masking each other and twisting in upon themselves. Opening a door like those hidden pictures in "Highlights Magazine" when I was nine. I studied each one until I had penetrated the camouflage. Without hesitation I crossed a threshold—those questions becoming my own. New questions unraveling within me. I wandered lost in a world of thought.

"Great exhibit!" James bounded back to where I was standing.

I flinched. He had seen the entire exhibit while I journeyed through the labyrinth of that single mask.

"I thought I'd lost you."

Perhaps he had. I wrenched myself away, but the mask gripped me like an insistent lover unwilling to end our clandestine affair. I looked down, wondering if James noticed any difference in me. The mask also seemed altered by our connection. Or was that my imagination? Would the staff notice the parts of me that stayed behind, see the changed shape of the lips forming the voiceless questions, note the color of the invisible eyes that peered out? Detect the lingering scent of yearning?

"All set?" His brusque query severed the link.

I took James's extended hand. We climbed the stairs to the courtyard where people milled about in small groups. Couples held hands, a young teenage girl sat with her family, eating cupcakes. Like thousands of visitors from around the world, I reached up to rub "The Thinker's" big toe. For luck. And to make a wish. A sugar-scented memory of my fourteenth birthday wafted in, the day I'd closed my eyes to make a wish—for Mom to be happier. As I opened them, my father blew my candles out before I could. He hooted with laughter, the alcohol on his breath a cloud around me. Mom re-lit the candles. The wish I made the second time was less kind. My first wish never came true. But the second one did—on my eighteenth birthday. Or maybe they both came true that day. If there is something that comes after this life, then maybe.

"What are you going to wish for?" James asked.

"Can't tell—wishes are supposed to be secret." I closed my eyes.

What to wish for . . . The word "Freedom" tugged at the hem of my consciousness. Freedom? I tried to pull away from the thought, to think of something more tangible. The concept kept tugging. Freedom from what?

Maybe I should wish for peace—inner peace. Although world peace would be a more commendable wish by Mom's only child. I squirmed, my inability to effect change nettling me like a thick wool coat—binding, heavy, itchy.

Maybe I should wish on the Thinker's toe to stop beating myself up. Or stop beating James up. Maybe I should wish that I wouldn't think so much—a blasphemous wish for the toe of the Thinker. "Be careful what you wish for," Mom's voice still echoed. Too many people didn't think clearly—or at all. I didn't want to join them. Perhaps a wish to forget my past, be able to move on from all the crap.

"You ready?"

Steam rose from twisted metal, the mental train wreck James's voice caused. Ready for what? Why was he always asking that? Ready to get going—move on—go fast—to what end?

I suddenly realized I was squeezing the Thinker's toe so hard my fingers were bruising. And I noticed a line waiting for a turn with the toe. I reassembled myself and applied a smile. "I guess so."

"I'm not trying to rush you, but the line was growing, and it looked like—"

"It's fine."

"I'm just . . . ready whenever you are." His sincerity made me feel more guilty.

"I'm ready." I summoned an energetic smile.

We unlocked our bikes, strapped on helmets, and mounted. "We'll cut back through the Marina then cross the bridge to the car. We can pick up take out on the way home."

James rode in the lead. We both preferred it that way: he liked to be out front, and it allowed my mind to wander. Sometimes his choice of direction or pace was frustrating, but I could follow with no risk of being told I had gone the wrong way or was going too slowly. James could always justify his choice, even in places we were exploring for the first time. No point arguing for spontaneity. I wasn't afraid of getting lost—I almost wished I could. Hopelessly lost. Slip into oblivion. The "Twilight Zone" theme danced through my brain.

Between the buildings along Cervantes Street, the commanding golden orange towers and cables of the Golden Gate Bridge rose up against the blue sky. Not surprising that people traveled around the world to see it, to walk across it, take pictures of it—even leap from it to almost certain death. How might one feel on the way down? Relief from whatever was so unbearable? Terror of the moments ahead? Regret that there was no way to hit "Undo"? Fear of drowning?

I saw James a block and a half ahead, pedaling urgently. I caught the sound of a baby crying—a newborn, faint but intensely personal. Heartbreaking. It pinched a long-buried nerve. My thoughts turned. The bike followed. Without making a decision, at Beach Street I simply turned left.

Everything shifted into soft focus, blurred around the edges. No conjecture about what was happening, just the pavement in front of me. Now. Now. Every second a new now. Each breath a new death, a new birth, a new death, a new birth. For the first time in my life, I was bereft of words. Only the experience itself existed. Time and space whizzing past unheeded. Simply being.

My pulse raced, my feet pressed hard against the pedals, something invisible dragging on me though the street was level and the air still. Oddly still. A dog barked somewhere.

A couple walked towards me on the opposite side of the street, holding hands. The woman glanced up. Our eyes locked. I was looking in a mirror, but a face not quite my own was reflected back. The mirror shattered. Echoed.

I rode on.

CHAPTER 2

Dog and Emmie

JAMES

As James rode up Cervantes Street, the Golden Gate Bridge was framed by houses on either side of the street painted in a spectrum of pastel colors. His eyes dropped to the pavement. The blur of the road surface was mesmerizing. His thoughts melted into the sound of his own breathing. Legs pumping, he forced it into an even rhythm. Core muscles working, sweating, sea air cleansing his lungs.

As he slowed for a stop sign, he heard a crash, like breaking glass. He hit the brakes hard, skidding to a halt. He looked around—no sign of an accident. No one nearby reacting to anything untoward. Ahead of him at the marina, masts of sailboats rocked rhythmically, ropes and hardware slapping and clanking like chimes. *Maybe that's all it was.*

He wasn't convinced.

Off to the left, the burnt orange of the Golden Gate Bridge against the solid blue sky, like a touched-up postcard photo, looked too perfect to be real. Couples strolled across a brilliant green lawn beneath elaborate kites that danced and twisted like wind marionettes. A teenager's three-sailed kite danced an exquisite solo around them. James recalled the summer he was ten. His dad had taken the brothers to the beach every weekend, kites and laughter soaring over the surf. Good times. Really good. That last summer with their dad. "God that takes me back! Cal and I used to . . ." He turned to look over his shoulder. Except for a few cars, the street was empty. *Something's wrong.* James scanned in every direction. His mind felt blurred. Suddenly his head ached. He struggled to discern what was so terribly wrong, but he couldn't think clearly.

Brushing it off as best he could, and hoping he wasn't having a heart attack—young, like his dad, he smiled uncertainly. If Cal had ever caught him talking to himself, he would have called his big brother a "looney bird," spiraling a finger around his ear. The memory of Cal eased his self-concern. It was probably just that—Cal.

James checked for cross traffic and rode onto the bike path, avoiding a tall blonde walking her dachshund. A thought stopped him: what had just happened? Why had he turned back? To whom had he been speaking when he turned? He nodded to an Asian woman with lush black hair ushering her small son safely across the bike path. He felt like he'd just awakened from a dream, *Maybe I was daydreaming, imagining Cal was alive and here.*

James tugged the shoulder strap on his backpack to make sure it was actually there. Yes—he could feel its weight. He tried to rationalize the unsettling feelings. *There are times we become so accustomed to something that we lose awareness of it. Not surprising, with so many other things demanding our attention.* Reaching back with his right elbow, he felt for the cool metal of his water bottle. He'd left many a water bottle in movie theaters. *No, it was bigger than that. What did I lose?* His throat thickened. *There was no loss worse than the one four years ago.*

An ominous sensation was creeping in—like the fog starting to roll in over the headlands. It spread, then clenched its fingers around his stomach. It felt like . . . *like the day I forgot to pick up Cal after school and got in big trouble. Whatever I lost, whatever I forgot—it was something important. I need to stop. To think.*

He veered off to find a grassy spot close to the water. Carefully leaning his bike against a pole, he pulled out a towel to sit on and a bag of home-made trail mix: pecans, almonds, chocolate chips, goji berries, and dried blueberries he'd picked up yesterday—*or was it the day before?* Not that it mattered, but a craving for certainty left him hungry for it.

From his right, a small dog bounded up pulling a young, strawberry-blond girl in a dress covered in large sunflowers, her green leggings like stems. The dog gave James a thorough nose-over. "Who are you?" the girl asked boldly.

"James."

"I'm Emmie. *That's* my mommy," pointing at a woman following far enough to give the child her space, but close enough to be protective. "This is Dog. She's part beagle. We don't know about the other part."

"What's her name?"

"Dog. I named her."

"That's very . . . clever. Well dubbed."

"What's dubbed?"

"Oh. Well, like when you dub a knight."

"It's not night. It's daytime."

"Yes, you are very astute."

"That's potty talk. Mommy says not to talk about toots."

"Toots? Oh, astute. Sorry. I meant you're being shrewd."

"I'm not the one being rude, you are," Emma insisted.

"I seem to keep digging myself deeper," James said, looking to Emmie's mom with a plea for help.

"Dog is a super-duper digger."

"I'm sure he is. Do you live around here?" James asked.

Emmie looked over at Mom, who shook her head. "I'm not allowed to tell cause you're a stranger until Mommy says you're not. I don't know when that is."

"Of course. I shouldn't have asked. I didn't think."

"Mommy is always telling me to think." Emmie leaned in to confess, "But it makes me tired out."

"Well, we're always thinking. When you talk, you're thinking."

"Nuh-uh. I'm just being. But I'm just almost five, so's I haven't learned to think all the time yet."

"Yeah, I guess that's a grown-up habit."

Dog lost interest in James and was tugging Emmie towards a bush ripe with dog news.

Mom stepped forward. "Emmie, let's leave the nice man alone. He probably wants to eat in peace."

James looked at the mom with auburn hair, unsure how to tell her how little he wanted to be alone right now.

"How do you know he's nice?" Emmie squinted up at her mother.

"Well, uh—we, uh—well, he seems to be a nice person."

Emmie studied her mom, head tipped all the way to one side, resisting Dog's tugs. "Does that mean he's not a stranger?"

"No, he is still a stranger, I just mean . . ." She turned, blushing, to James. "Sorry to have disturbed you, sir."

"It's fine. No need to apologize."

Like a Sherlock Holmes with Dr. Watson unable to keep pace behind him, Dog tugged Emmie away. "She doesn't think about how other people—"

"Really, it was . . . very sweet. Her hair is just like my daughter's when she was . . ."

Where did that *come from! Was that a pick-up line? I don't have a daughter. . . .* Fog wrapped itself around that thought, rendering James oddly uncertain about himself and his reality. He'd set himself a trap. Prayed she wouldn't delve, not wanting to lose his tenuous connection to this attractive woman. "Would you like to sit? Dog seems quite busy there."

Mom looked uncertain. Feeling awkward, he stood up. "I'm James. And . . . I am nice. I mean, I try to be." Her left hand went to a delicate hourglass pendant with sage colored sand that she wore on a thin gold chain. James noted the lack of ring.

"Okay." Facing Emmie, she sat on the edge of James's towel.

She wore brown denim pants and a pullover fleece top that perfectly matched her pendant. James scooted to the far end of the towel, leaving as much space as possible between them. He noticed how ragged the towel was and wondered if he was making a wretched first impression—or if perhaps she was the practical type who wouldn't use "good" towels at the park.

He held up his bag of trail mix, regretting not packing it in something more reusable, like a deli container. People in the Bay Area were said to be more environmentally conscious than in the Midwest.

Dog and Emmie raced over. Dog poked his nose toward the nut bag, and Emmie asked, "Is he still a stranger, Mommy? Or something else?"

Dog whipped around before Mommy could answer, dragging Emmie after a small poodle. Mommy got up quickly and called, "Sorry."

They were out of earshot before James thought to call out, "What's your name?!" He heard Emmie's laughter on the brisk Bay wind—the same wind that kept his question from reaching Emmie's mother.

Absent-mindedly chomping dried blueberries, James worked over his stupid blurt about having a daughter. He closed his eyes. Emmie had triggered something—but the harder he tried to find it, the further away it swam. Frustration swelled. Splashing sounds diverted him. His mind replayed the memory of playing blind tag in the swimming pool with Cal. Eyes closed, he shouted "Marco," and listened for Cal's response to know which direction to swim in pursuit. "Polo! You'll never catch me, Jimmy!" Splash and silence. James gave up and opened his eyes. Kids were throwing rocks into the water. The Marina scene was beautiful minutes ago, but now his world was upside down.

In a surge of anger, James wrapped the twist tie around his baggie and flung it into his backpack. He yanked the zipper to close it. "Goddamnit!" It jammed on a loose thread. He jerked it repeatedly, until in fury, he pulled out his pocketknife and poked at the thread. The knife slipped, nicking his left thumb. "Fuck!" He dropped his knife and squeezed his thumb hard. Blood dripped on the grass. He wrapped the towel around his thumb so he wouldn't see the blood. Across the park, Dog and Emmie were running, her blond curls bouncing in the sun. James swayed, puzzling over the kaleidoscopic scene.

In his backpack, he found a beat-up bandage and applied it awkwardly. Shoving the towel into his pack, he wrestled the zipper closed, and flipped the pack onto his back.

Fog pouring in over the headlands, as dense as an eider down, he mounted and rode along Crissy Field. Maybe he'd pick up a movie on the way home. Films were his escape of choice—plus screen time before bed. The drawback was returning to the real world at the end, restless and itchy to move on, to move out. It's what he liked about his job—short assignments and frequent moves.

As he sped west on the bike path toward some huge orange metal sculptures, he thought about this most recent move. The details escaped his recall. He reasoned that was probably because the company always handled most of them. He would lay out the kind of rental he would like—within reason, of course, then show up with his toothbrush. At times it was too easy, leaving his mind free to ruminate on details of his life he wished he could revise. If he had to deal with more of his present life, perhaps his past would quiet down and leave him alone.

He was slowed by the migration of a crowd. He intercepted a plump fiftyish woman carrying a folding lawn chair. "Excuse me. What's happening?"

"It's a musical piece written for eight hundred musicians. Starting at 4:00." She lumbered on, shifting her bulk from one leg to the other.

James checked his watch: 3:56. He walked his bike to the nexus of activity. School bands with adult conductors were clumped around the park: full orchestras, drum corps, strings, brass bands, vocalists, some with instruments James didn't recognize. The crowd wandered and chatted as the groups played a kind of harmonious cacophony carved out of salt wind—organized chaos gathering and scattering, whispering promises while breaking them. He felt an urge to merge into this experience. Surrounded by people, he felt terribly alone. Yet he sensed a tenuous connection among them forming out of the sculpted sound and shared experience. But then their faces flattened and grayed like an old photo, blurring. His thumb throbbed in his clenched fist. He looked down at it. Blood seeped through the bandage, carrying with it unbidden memories.

Bloodied bandages. At the hospital, waiting, standing by the bed—unable to sit. Short irregular breaths catching in his throat, tears imprisoned behind bars of sheer will. Screaming silently. Hoping without believing that everything would turn out the way it should. Angry at someone, everyone, himself. God. *If He exists.*

A single sharp drumbeat yanked him back to the present. A breath caught in his chest—poised for danger. James chided himself for still allowing the sight of blood to hijack him. The drum corps moved closer, the conductor stabbing his baton at an invisible adversary. Beats like shots pounded into him. James backed away. A dozen electric guitars oozed a piercing wail which pushed James like the paddle of a pinball machine toward vocalists, keening into the space around, between, and in and out of the crowd of bodies—directly into him. The sound lodged in his stomach and throat.

"Are you okay?" A woman was looking at him with concern. She pointed at his injured hand held tight to his stomach. Suddenly, she was the only other person on the field, his brittle awareness splintering off from the crowd so he could focus on her.

He replayed her question before answering. He didn't know if he was okay—probably not—but he wasn't even certain what that might mean. Perhaps her answer would help him find his own.

"Are you?" he asked blankly.

"Intense, isn't it?" She smiled. He nodded. "Looks like you might need to change that bandage soon." James looked at his thumb, then back at her. "I have some if you need one."

James started breathing again. "Yes, thanks. I didn't come prepared. Wasn't expecting . . ."

She laughed kindly. "If you were expecting it, that would probably not be a good sign. Here." The woman dug in her purse. She pulled out bandages and latex gloves. "I was a Girl Scout. Always prepared. Now I'm a nurse. You want me to . . . ?"

"Sure, thanks." James watched her hazel eyes focused on the task. She looked up, wrapping the old bandage inside the gloves as she snapped them off inside out. James smiled. "Very professional! Thanks."

"You're welcome." She waved to someone across the field. "That's my wife." A mocha-skinned woman ran over and kissed her. "Hey, babe. This is—sorry, I didn't catch your name."

"James."

"This is Janelle. I'm Janet."

Janelle extended a hand, saw the gloves and the bandage on James's thumb. "You playing nurse again? My personal Mother Theresa. God, I love you." They kissed again. "We gotta go. They're holding a table for us, and I promised we'd get there before the waitress came back for our order."

Janet laughed. "Completely impossible."

"Bend time, baby. I keep telling you: time is merely a mental construct. I'm never late for anything. I can't be—unless I decide to be. I'm always right on time."

Janet rolled her eyes. James liked their easy laughter. "Totally crazy and I totally love her for it. Nice meeting you, James. I guess we're off to bend some time." They skipped down the meadow, arms swinging together in harmony.

"Bye!" James called after them. "Thanks!" They laughed and waved. He unconsciously leaned forward to taste their double scoop of joy and peace. But they were gone.

The bands had spread out across the field. The audience had also dispersed as the fog obliterated the Marin hills. The sun was low, and a chilly wind was picking up. James downed a slug of water and rode back toward the bike path that led to the majestic bridge.

Bikers sailed down the other side of the street. He dropped gears quickly as the incline steepened. His heart pounded and muscles ached. Frustrated by his lack of progress, he dropped his feet to the ground and pounded the handlebars. *Damn it all!*

A cry up ahead distracted him from his temper tantrum. At a sharp bend in the road, a man paused to soothe the distressed infant snuggled against his chest. The mother rounded the bend in a jog and lifted the crying baby from the pack. Carrying the bundle to a fallen tree, she sat and adjusted her shirt for nursing. The father stood guard, blocking the view of his family. Protective. Attentive.

A wave of guilt, like nausea, rolled through James, carrying with it a punishing surge of failed responsibility. He summoned a smile, nodded to the father. James's dad had had a bearing like that—protector. As he resumed riding, James thought maybe he had been delivered a message—or a new perspective. He stopped at the overlook to read about the construction of the bridge, though he registered only something about how its flexibility made it possible to withstand nearly a century of salt water and wind. Something about surviving, about holding up under the strain.

A collage formed—the breathtaking view; a baby safely cared for; a hill defeating a man; a dead tree providing a seat for a nursing mother; a bridge holding up. James felt chilled, needed something hot. He rode toward the bridge and the cafe, focused on coffee. Black. Hot. The chill inside arose from a depth that unnerved him.

He locked up the bike and entered the exuberant crowd

inside—a solitary boat adrift in a sea of activity and chatter. It made him desperate to be physically alone again. *I need a movie. To disappear.* Exiting quickly, he crossed under, then up to the west side of the bridge reserved for bikers. He pedaled hard, the sea wind challenging him. *Can't catch me, Jimmy,* his little brother's voice taunted. *Yes, I can!* Overtaking rider after rider, he raced forward, the wind wiping the tears from his cheeks.

He strapped the bike onto the rack and started the car. A scent, familiar yet indistinct, hovered like a ghost. Again: the sensation of having forgotten something important. He put the car in reverse. "Ready?" he asked the ghost. He drove north to leave it all behind, not caring what movie was playing when he arrived at the theater.

CHAPTER 3

Coconut Dreams

HANNAH

Sitting in the tiny living room in what Maudie called *the olive*—a green stuffed easy chair with a pimento-colored pillow—Hannah pulled a stash of books from her backpack. All books she had read. That alone creeped her out. But the last one, a journal with a soft brown moleskin cover threatened like a dark doorway. More terrifying for its sense of familiarity. She took a deep breath and slipped off the elastic that held it closed.

She was still trying to figure out what had happened twenty-six days ago. She'd been on her bike—nothing odd about that. A fear niggled, chewing on her like a termite in the structural beam of her existence, that the absence of short-term memory signaled something serious. Like early-onset dementia or some trauma so horrific she'd blocked it out—the brain's built-in protective system kicking in. Attempted rape? Mugging? She didn't have any bruises to suggest a physical struggle. She was sure of her name, at least—*thank God!* Apparently, she had published a cookbook specializing in baked desserts. She thought through how she'd retrieved that piece:

Friday, October 11, 2012. I was riding my bike, must have gotten lost. I was shaken, like I was running away from some horrific event—desperate. Walking Ruby up 23rd Avenue, heading south—as far as I could tell in the fog, I was parched, took a gulp from my water bottle. As I tilted my head back, I noticed a crooked sign in an upstairs window: "Room for Rent." Almost hidden behind an ornamental plum tree still leaf-clad, defying the season.

It hit me then that I would need a place to sleep. My jacket was lightweight, offering little protection against the cold. There wasn't much in my backpack aside from a small blank notepad and pencil, some protein bar wrappers, and a now-empty bag of homemade trail mix. Not even my cell phone—which seemed particularly weird.

I stared at the sign, a feeling of trepidation descending. Rent. I'd have to fill out an application. That would mean questions. I had more of those myself than I could deal with and virtually no answers to go with them. Moving in immediately with nothing but my bike and daypack? Even if I could find a cheap hotel—with no ID or credit cards and just sixty-two dollars in cash—what were the odds they'd even let me stay? How was I going to convince anyone to trust that I'd pay? Even I didn't know how that would happen.

I could go to the police. A feeling of guilt rejected that suggestion. What if I'd blocked out an act I'd perpetrated? I needed time to sort it out, figure out what happened to me. I just needed a short-term solution. I looked again at the sign.

What might the landlord think: a convict on the run?

An abused wife, husband close behind?

A homeless bum? Fiction crashed into fiction, piling up at my feet, imagined reasons for this non-fictional situation littering the path in front of me.

Frankly, I was—as Mom had often complained—a book-aholic. What would the landlord make of this non-fiction oddity on his doorstep?

And was I even non-fiction? My life felt like drafts of a novel in revision, missing scenes essential to the story, clearly in need of a structural editor. My right knee was starting to stiffen up, remnant of a car accident. There was some solace in that high school memory. My past wasn't a complete blank. Mom was there too.

I focused on Mom, snuggled up to the memory of her warmth. She had tried so hard. I guess Dad had too, but the only way he knew to feel good about himself was to put everyone else down. Yet in this moment, even memories of his insults and taunts were a comfort. At least a foundation. I probed for more details, even prodding the pain of his verbal abuse. I could only get as far as age eighteen. Apparently even if my mind could erase decades, I would never be free of the memory of the Big Decision.

Feeling fragmented, I rode around the corner and down a fairly level block hoping to return with a clear story. Shouldn't be too hard for a writer. I braked and stopped. I'm a writer. Yes, that felt true. But what did I write?

It was getting dark. I had to take the plunge. I turned around and coasted back to the blue house. The sign was still in the window—a fluke that I'd even seen it. I locked my bike to a "No Parking" sign, enjoying the irony.

Eight steep steps to the front door. I pushed the doorbell but didn't hear it ring. I waited, shivering, unsure whether to knock. Maybe the landlord was old or infirm. The stairs indicated not. I waited a minute more, then knocked loudly.

"Coming!" A woman's voice. Realizing I had my helmet on, I unsnapped the buckle and smoothed my hair, damp from the ride and my nerves. I sniffed my armpit. Best to maintain some personal space.

Another full minute passed. Perhaps the voice had said, "Come in." Unlikely in any city both that the front door might be unlocked and a woman would invite someone in like that. Maybe in some small Midwest town, but not a city.

I was just turning to go when the door opened wide. A round woman with chocolate brown skin and graying hair, wearing a checkered apron dusted with flour and splotched with what looked like raspberries, held a hand mixer on the verge of dripping something creamy onto the floorboards. We stood, each absorbing the unexpected sight of the other in silence.

"Hi," I said as the first glob hit the floor. We both looked down. The woman looked at the mixer, then turned and left. Feeling responsible *for the glob, my eyes remained fixed on it. It had the consistency more of dough than of batter. I wondered whether it was sweet or savory. I guessed sweet. My nose confirmed. Definitely chocolate, with a hint of coconut. My favorite combination.*

My empty stomach growled at me. The glob was starting to look appetizing. The woman returned with a damp paper towel, swiped the glob, scrunched the towel, and looked up. "Yes?"

"Sorry to interrupt. Looks like you're baking. I noticed the sign about the room," *I pointed up,* "and . . ." *The woman tilted her head as if perplexed.* "I'm looking for a room." *She tilted her head the other way.* "If it's still available . . ." *This wasn't going well. I felt like slinking away but had nowhere to slink to.*

The woman walked past me out into the street, turned and looked at her upstairs window. "For heaven's sake." *A green BMW coming down the block didn't slow. I was about to shout when the driver swerved around her. Oblivious, she climbed the steps and resumed her position facing me.* "Well, I guess you better come in then."

"Oh. Thanks." *Even a short respite from the cold would make the upcoming inquisition worth it.*

A timer dinged in the next room. "Oh, Lord!" *The woman dashed off to the right through an archway. I closed the door and waited, uncertain about the polite course of action. I heard an oven door drop open, a pan sliding out, the clang of a cooling rack, the scrape of a spatula. Then the potent aroma of hot cookies—sounds and smells of a familiar, comforting world—filled the entry hall where I waited. My shoulders relaxed as I was transported to my mother's kitchen. We had always loved discovering great recipes and making up new ones. It had been the beginning of my . . .*

"Where are you?" *the woman's voice echoed down the hall behind the aroma.*

"Still here."

"Well, come on in here so we can talk." *My nose led me to the compact but well laid out kitchen with yellow walls, wooden cabinets and drawers, a six-burner Wedgewood stove with a double oven,* and small counters on either side crowded with bowls, measuring cups and spoons, whole wheat flour. A book lay open beside a bag of coconut sugar. "You're just in time. Have a seat." She pointed with Christmassy holly-patterned oven mitts to a small table with two chairs. "You want milk?"

This took me completely by surprise. "No, thank you."

"Lactose intolerant?"

"A bit."

"So many folks are. I got almond milk?"

"Really?" I was hesitant to impose but was famished. "That would be great." The interview was off to a great start.

She poured two glasses of almond milk, retrieved small china plates from a cabinet, and slid two cookies onto each one. We sat across the table from each other. I tried to make the cookie feast last, while hopefully avoiding the impression of homelessness. But the hunger in me pulled against its leash. It growled—loudly.

I could feel her examining me. "Delicious," I said, the compliment genuine.

"Do I know you?" she asked as I pressed the last crumbs with my finger to collect them. "Help yourself to another."

Almost apologetically, I took a third. "Thanks, they ARE delicious. I . . . I don't think so."

"You look familiar somehow."

I savored the familiar confection. "Is the room still available?"

"That's another thing. Well, I mean, yes, but . . ." My heart sank—she didn't want to rent to someone looking—and smelling—like me.

"I'm sorry to have troubled you. It was very kind of you to . . ." I didn't want to say, "feed me." That would certainly make me seem homeless. I hoped my vague gestures would suffice. I rose to leave.

"I thought you needed a room."

"I do. I thought . . ."

"Maybe you better stop thinking an' set yourself down an' have yourself another cookie. I can tell you're hungry. No shame in hunger. Happens to all of us every day. Besides, if I eat all these myself, I'll just *get rounder than I already am. I bake for the fun of it, but then I'm surrounded by temptation.* Lead me not into temptation. *I have yet to get an answer to that prayer. Me being more of a sweet-by-and-by kind of girl, I would buy and buy and buy sweets. I thought it might help if I started baking without so much sugar, so I just bought this cookbook that calls for less of it and for different kinds of sweeteners."* She picked up the cookbook, flipped the back cover closed. And gasped. She looked at me again. *"Lord have mercy, it's you! Hannah Fleet! You wrote this book!* Hannah Fleet's Better Eats!"

I smiled, surprised as she was. *Good to know that I wrote cookbooks—and was even published! "Thank you. Thank you so much!"* She probably thought I was thanking her for the compliment, but it was for the revelation.

"I love this book! These are the Toasted Coconut Dreams—but of course you'd already know that! Of course you'd know." Suddenly the woman was frowning at her cookies. *"Are they okay? Your recipes are so clear, but I'm no pro. An' here I am serving you somethin' right out of your own book."* She shook her head.

"They're perfect," I assured her. And they were.

She pulled the rack of cooling cookies between us, and we each took another. *"Hannah Fleet, New York Times best-selling author. Here in my kitchen! I am so honored!"*

I was starting to feel like a fraud—a grateful fraud. Hoping to duck out of the spotlight, I began again, "The room . . ."

The landlady sat back. *"That's another funny thing. By the way, I'm Maudie Farrow."*

"Nice to meet you, Maudie." We shook hands.

"It's a funny thing. About the room. I haven't had anybody rentin' for some time now, but I been thinkin' I should get someone in. Gets lonely on my own sometimes, you know. Nice to have another woman around. Someone to share cookies with." We shared a smile. *"But I hadn't gotten round to doing anythin' about it yet."*

"Except the sign."

"No, not even that. That's what's so bafflin'. I haven't even used

that sign in . . . oh, maybe fifteen years or so. Craigslist is the way to go these days. I had a woman friend rentin' for eleven years. But she went off to take care of her dyin' mother. I just let the room sit, thinkin' maybe she'd return someday. I expect she just stayed on after her mother passed, the house now hers. Just today' I thought I'd write up a listin', but then I got to browsin' your book over coffee—and these Toasted Coconut Dreams looked so mmm-mmm. I had all the ingredients, so I started bakin', and then the knock on the door—did you ring? The bell doesn't work, hasn't since before I can remember."

"I did."

"Good thing you knocked. I was just gettin' the last tray popped in, which is why . . ." The timer interrupted. Maudie pulled out the last tray of cookies, slid them onto a second cooling rack, turned off the oven, and added the cookie sheet to the pile in the sink. "When would you like to move in?"

I hesitated. I'd expected to endure questions and confrontations and rejections. To have to tell partial truths and fill out an application. This was so easy, maybe I was making a mistake—being gullible, not on alert for danger? I looked at the cookies, picked up another, and faced Maudie. "Now?"

Maudie burst out laughing, as if I were joking. She appeared to travel the mental landscape I'd just vacated. "Great! Welcome home, Hannah Fleet." We simultaneously bit into another cookie to confirm our agreement. "Got any stuff?"

"Just me and Ruby."

Maudie's face fell. "Ruby? Now, I got no problem with you bein' a lesbian, but it's just a single room . . ."

"My bike—I call her Ruby."

Maudie brightened again. "Alrighty then. I have an extra tooth-brush if you need one."

"And . . . rent? I'm kind of between . . ."

Maudie had studied me, the best-selling author with no stuff who sat in her kitchen. She'd apparently learned to trust her instincts. Could she sense this moment was pivotal for me, detect in my eyes the fear I was trying to hide? "First week stay as my guest. Let's see how it works out."

A breath escaped. I hadn't realized I'd been holding it. I must be dreaming—but this time it was a good dream. I smiled, hoping not to wake up too soon.

In the days that followed that kitchen meeting, Hannah spent hours in the local library, Googling her name, searching for information about herself. But what she found didn't feel *right*—didn't feel like a life she had been living. When Maudie went off to work, Hannah would read the book she supposedly wrote, trying to make sense of it. All the references to her daughter—how could that be? It was impossible. She better than anyone knew there was no child. Did she make it up for the sake of the book? Wishful thinking? Or was she a carbon copy of this author but without the exact same history? The few childhood references matched up with memory, but it wasn't much to go on. How much could she even trust those?

A few days earlier, Hannah had tracked down the cookbook publisher. Hoping it would not turn out to be a huge mistake, she'd called and been connected to Michelle.

"Hey there, Hannah, good to hear from you. You get settled in your new place? I'm jealous. I love San Francisco." It sounded like Michelle was eating lunch by the crinkling of the deli paper. It would be noon Eastern Time. Her voice sounded familiar—*a good sign.*

"Ah, sort of. I just wanted to make sure you had the address."

"Yep, you sent it to me before you moved. We're up to date. Unless something else has changed."

"No. That's great. Maybe . . . just to be sure . . . what's the address I gave you?" She grabbed her pen and notepad.

"Sure. Hang on." Hannah could hear a keyboard clacking. "We've got 2418 Quintara Street, San Francisco, 94116."

"Great, that's right. Thanks."

There was a short silence. "You okay? You sound a little . . . more anxious than usual, and that's saying something."

"Fine. You know, change is . . . you know . . ." Hannah trailed off.

"Moving is hell. But seemed like the change would be good for you two. I hope that plays out."

"Us two?"

"You and Bob. Last time we talked, things seemed a little rocky."

"Right, Bob . . . yeah, well . . . we'll see."

"It's none of my business, but I care about you. If you ask me—which I know you didn't—but he's not good enough for you. You deserve better."

"Thanks."

"Hey, I gotta run, but I'm glad you called, Hannah. Oh, and remember to send over your new banking info so we can get royalties out to you. We've been holding them during the move like you asked. We'll talk soon."

Like an investigative reporter, Hannah jumped on her bike to find the address. There was a "For Rent" sign in that window. She didn't have a phone yet, so she wrote down the number and raced back to use the archaic wall phone at Maudie's. The landlord was happy to show it ASAP. Hannah returned at 1:00, nervous about the possibility of recognition and not sure what that could lead to.

She stood on the bottom step as he unlocked the door. "A guy moving to town rented it long distance but moved out after the first month. He told me his girl ditched him their first week here and he didn't want her coming back to find him. Said he had a girl on the side anyway, so he didn't need it anymore." He gave a half smile. "Maybe that's why the girl ditched him. Here we go." The door swung open and she followed him in. "Nothing wrong with the apartment—just the jerk who rented it. I can make you a deal for the first month if you want it."

It was small and open plan, obviously renovated, with just the bedroom and bathroom having doors for privacy. In the bedroom, Hannah caught sight of a handful of books on the closet shelf. All familiar.

"Sorry, thought I'd cleared everything out. Guess I missed those."

"I love books." Hannah ran her fingers over the spines.

"You're welcome to them."

"Sure, if you don't mind. What was the guy's name?"

The landlord looked at her sideways. "You a reporter or cop or something?"

"No, sorry, just curious. I'm a writer, didn't mean to pry. I'll take an application, but I'll have to give notice where I am now . . . so, not sure if the timing will be right." He looked disappointed but pulled out an application and handed it to her. "Nice place. Thanks for showing it on such short notice."

"A writer, huh?"

She nodded as she stuffed the books into her backpack.

"Novels?"

"Cookbook. I'd like to write a novel—still coming up with a plot."

"Cool. I facilitate a book club in the neighborhood. Mostly murder mysteries."

"That's what I've been thinking about writing, a series with a food theme, like Killer Menu or something."

"Great title! Hey, if you want to join us sometime, let me know. You have my number."

"That might be nice. Thanks."

"What's your name? I don't think you said."

"Hannah. I gotta run. Thanks."

As she unlocked her bike, he called out to her. "Bob!"

"What?"

"The guy's name was Bob."

She clipped her left shoe in and swung her leg over Ruby in a panic.

At Maudie's she set aside the stack of books and cautiously opened the journal she'd pulled from her backpack. It began *"Prologue. I turned left. . . ."*

CHAPTER 4

W-Hole-ness

JAMES

As if all thought had fallen into the dark, empty hole at his feet, James stood blankly. Time ceased to exist—briefly. Except that *brief* can only exist when time does. Like eternity. Or perhaps eternity is the absence of time. James was beyond time, but still in Marin on Mount Tamalpais . . . until a furry brown head kick-started time with a jolt as a gopher popped up to check on things topside.

A phrase from the trailer for *What the Bleep Do We Know?* drifted into a pocket of his mind like a dandelion seed: *How far down the rabbit hole do you want to go?* He looked out over the valley, judging the hour by the sun's position. *I should head back. Odd—it's October, but warm like some other season. What with climate change, normal isn't normal anymore.* "I don't think we're in Kansas anymore, Toto," he said to the gopher. "Planet Earth seems to have left Kansas."

Life used to be filled with things you could count on. When you were a kid, you went to school and griped about homework and played with friends. Holidays and vacations that broke up the year. There were new bikes and ice cream sundaes and favorite toys that got lost or were taken away—for misbehavior or by other misbehaving kids. Growing up meant increasing responsibilities, finding employment, maybe a partner and kids. Something tightened inside. He swallowed hard.

Tears blurred his view over the valley. A thought of Emmie, the little sunflower girl from the Marina, invoked technicolor memories of family life: loud meals around the table, playing frisbee, holidays, getting in trouble . . . good times. And something else hiding in the background, out of focus. A baby strapped in a car seat. An angry mother. Guilt.

The vacated gopher hole stirred up another emptiness that plagued him. Cal, with his talent for either cheering him up or pissing him off, would have told him he needed to get laid.

Four years ago today, November 12, 2009, a hole in Cal's gut became a hole in James's life. In the wake of events, James couldn't fully recall the argument that set it off. In a rage, Cal took off to the American River, where he pissed off some big, tattooed guy just out on parole. Two angry men meeting in the woods sounded like the beginning of a bad joke, but the shot that cut through the roar of the raging river below them was hardly a joke. The river continued to rage, but Cal had only pain and fear and regret. Their argument? Whatever it was, it was stupid. Pointless.

The crack of the shot and wheels spinning out as the other guy took off had interrupted a woman meditating on the riverbank. She had slipped on her shoes and found Cal, his cell phone six inches above the bullet hole. She'd called 911, then the number of the last person Cal had called: *Big Bro*. Cal never used a password on his phone—he trusted everyone.

Two hours later, James was clinging to Cal's right hand tightly to keep him from slipping away. Every word James formulated seemed trivial, ridiculous. Tears were flowing down his cheeks as Cal's eyes closed and the hand went limp. Cal's final words were not tombstone material: *Stupid. Shit.*

"I'm sorry!" James exploded, squeezing Cal's hand, expecting his brother to tell him to shut up. "I'm sorry," he whispered hoarsely. "I'm sorry. I'm so sorry . . ." Cal's mouth had dropped open. Breath-less. Bottomless. Empty. Still. James stared into that dark hole.

The gopher reappeared, looked directly at James. Time faltered.

James trudged hard up a steep incline hoping to find a modicum of peace before he headed back to the house, uncertain he'd ever experience such a thing again.

Cal's boy-voice rang in his head. "Do-over! Do-over!" As a bossy big-brother he called back, "No way, Cal—you messed up. Too late now." Cal's frustration had given James a sense of power back then. If their mom had heard him, she would've reminded him that Cal wasn't like other kids—he needed James to protect him, help him understand social cues.

If I hadn't been such a jerk, Cal would be here, beside me, enjoying the vista. Do-over! he shouted to whoever could change the rules. But no one was in charge. No God, no universal power. Just stupid, miserable humans scrabbling to make it to the end of the race with as little pain as possible. The rules would never change. Cal was gone. They were all gone.

Like dominoes their family had fallen: his baby sister didn't live past two, a loss that tortured his father with guilt—even though it was an accident and no one else blamed him. After his father's heart attack, it was Mom, then Cal. James was the only one left.

As James scanned the hill's dry brown grass flattened by hikers like himself on a narrow path, he tried to recall life before that day in the emergency room—its ease and familiarity, complacency, bright colors. So ephemeral. Why does anything matter—it won't last. To escape these shadows, James had immersed himself in work, always looking to the next something to avoid dealing with how much Now was not like Before. He could put on a happy demeanor like a coat, wear a smile when others were around—in memory of Cal and his naïve, infectious smile. *I owe him at least that.*

He tripped on a root sticking up in the trail. His eyes landed on a flat rock, and his knees on the tall dry grass. Breathing heavily, he heaved himself onto the rock, removed his pack and scanned the view. A red-tailed hawk perched on the top branch of an oak stared down at him. "Why are you looking at me like that? We're on the same end of the food chain." A slithering drew his eyes to a skittish lizard. "Someone wants to invite you out for lunch."

James looked between them. From the raptor's perspective, James was an obstruction. From the lizard's, he was a savior.

Are we each seeing the world from our own perch? He had a vague memory of a young woman with reddish gold hair going on about perspective and how blind he was to hers. *Could there be a perspective from which it was* not *unfair that Cal had died? To the bird is it unfair that I'm blocking lunch? Is it torn apart by anger and anguish and loss about it? Of course not. But then, birds supposedly don't have much emotional range, nor thoughts about past or future. They're as stuck in the Now as I'm stuck in the past.*

I wonder if I could just focus on Now instead of the pain. It's a beautiful day. I'm out hiking, which I enjoy. I'm not hungry, the weather's pleasant, my body's resting. But Cal's death held him tightly, clenched in its fist of justified rage. "Lucky fuckin' bird," he muttered. The hawk's gaze shifted slightly, giving James the distinct feeling that it was now looking at him in earnest. "Okay—I get it. Maybe I have a choice. At least I can try."

The lizard scurried and the raptor swooped towards them. James ducked low and felt the breeze of its enormous wings. When he stood up, both creatures had vanished. He searched the sky. *Did I imagine it all?*

If so, did that make it any less real?

The sun slipped behind the hill, reminding him that daylight would end soon. He took a swig of water and swung the pack into place as a flock of wild turkeys strutted into view below him. "You guys should be in hiding—Thanksgiving is just around the corner." They made gobbling noises as they fled from him, heads jerking forward and back with each rapid step.

James stretched his hand out in front of him, fingers spread, trying to match the shape of his hand to their plump bodies. In elementary school he'd traced his hand on construction paper for a laminated turkey placemat. Cal had too. For years their mother set Thanksgiving dinner on them, in spite of objections in their middle and high school years. After she passed, they found them in a box in her condo. He and Cal joked about burying them with her. Now James wished he'd kept them—Cal's at least.

He wrestled with the fear that over time he'd forget his brother's face. Too busy living life to think about memorializing it, neither had bothered with photos. He'd expected to tease Cal about gray hair and wrinkles, tell nieces and nephews embarrassing stories about their dad. But Cal died without a wife or kids.

James hadn't married either, though he'd come close once, back when he was young and stupider. Some people lived with the fear of what might happen, but he lived with the pain of what never would. His mind drifted back to college, to meeting Hannah. *We were kids ourselves, too young to . . .* The thought slammed into a barricade. Dusk was settling in.

Suddenly he was frantic to get off this hill and back to the house. He moved quickly on the dry, narrow path down the hill towards the lit windows and glowing streetlamps below. A rabbit dashed away to his left. He paused briefly as he caught sight of a skunk waddling towards a rotting log, home to grubs as the earth reclaimed the fallen oak. Dust to dust.

James felt the itch of a tear leaving a trail in the dust on his right cheek. He didn't stop to wipe it away.

CHAPTER 5

In Between

HANNAH

The morning air was so nippy that Hannah could see the trail of her breath as she startled awake. She tugged the comforter tighter around her neck. "I sleep better with the heat off at night, no matter how low the temperature," Maudie had declared, handing Hannah a thick down duvet. Its cover, obviously designed for college students, displayed a spreadsheet timetable of classes and activities. The suggestion of order within clean boundaries was soothing.

Hannah's father had refused to let Mom turn up the thermostat in winter. Under a pile of heavy wool blankets, she lay immobilized as she said goodnight. But as soon as the door clicked shut, she wrestled them loose enough to breathe again. Her best friend had a down comforter, but Hannah dared not ask for one. Her father could afford it but insisted there was no need to be wasteful. When he was comfortable, the temperature was fine—everyone else should just deal with it. What a treat to climb into bed each night to snuggle under this warm cloud!

Unsettled by a dream, she saw 4:45 on the LED display. Waking early was part of her new routine, though she had a feeling she was previously a night owl. Routine eased her anxiety.

The journal from the apartment on Quintara Street freaked Hannah out. Something strange was going on—not early dementia, nor trauma blotting out memory, nor even a brain glitch explained that journal. Someone, who was not her—she was pretty sure it wasn't hers even though the handwriting was—had started writing a story that *felt* like her life, though not a life she was living—like an autobiography that needed some serious fact-checking.

But if she *had* written it, where had that life's memories disappeared to? *I grew up in New Jersey. That feels solid. But after Grandma died and James and I . . .* James! *Could it be the same James? Then who is Bob? And how could I be living with James in San Rafael and Bob in San Francisco at the same time? This is not dementia. Maybe schizophrenia! But that would all be in my head, so what about the other people involved here? Maybe this is what it would be like to have a clone. Or live in a parallel universe?*

But Hannah didn't buy any of these stories. No explanation made any sense, and there was no one she dared talk to about it. An unnerving suggestion quivered at the edge of her thoughts. Her mom pointed at it with her I-told-you-so look. After a lifelong yearning to disappear into a world of fiction, Hannah was starting to fear she actually had.

But even that didn't make sense.

A few weeks ago, Hannah had snuck a peek at Maudie's book on quantum physics, was surprised that her down-to-earth, kitchen-loving landlady—*friend*, she corrected herself—would read anything that sounded so dry. But the introduction grabbed her. Now she was hooked too. *At the tiniest nano level are waves of possibility—until you observe them. Then, bam, they snap into particle form and become reality. Weird—yet cool. If reality can be that amorphous, things may not be what they seem. Maybe it's not just me that's left orbit.*

Hannah pulled the mysterious journal under the comforter. Except for the Prologue and Chapter One, the rest of the thick journal was blank. Inviting her. She grabbed a mechanical pencil from the nightstand and added: *Am I a particle—or a wave?*

Before the alarm buzzed, she shut it off, pulled on her clothes and two pairs of socks. She dropped the journal and pencil into her backpack. *The possibility of a hot drink is a wave of potential I can surf, until it shows up in my hands as a particle.* She slipped quietly down to the kitchen.

"Mornin'," Maudie called.

"Morning."

"Sleep well?"

"Woke up from a dream."

"Dreams are good."

"Maybe yours are." The flame already lit under the kettle, Hannah slipped into a chair.

"You remember it?" Maudie asked without looking up.

"Parts. I walked into this dark cave. Couldn't see where I was going, but I just kept walking forward into the dark. I don't really like the dark."

"Can't have light if you don't have dark," Maudie chirped.

Hannah paused.

"No use denyin' it, even if you don't wanna accept it. What happened next?" The kettle whistled and Maudie poured hot water into two large mugs.

Hannah took her tea in both hands to warm them, "I heard a young girl calling me, like she needed help. It felt like I was her mom, but I didn't know where she was."

"Hmm." Maudie stirred her tea.

"I've had dreams like that before. I mean, they kind of make sense." Maudie looked up questioningly. "I got pregnant when I was a teenager. Didn't know what to do. My parents were dead. I had no support system. Nothing. And the father was . . . oh my God." Hannah's eyes darted around, wheels spinning wildly in her head as another puzzle piece snapped into place.

"What? You look white as a ghost."

"His name was James."

Maudie paused then laughed. "Well, that's a pretty common name. What's wrong with him being named James?"

Hannah took a gulp of the hot tea. It burned on the way down. "Nothing. I was just thinking I need to get moving or I'll be late."

"Girl, you got plenty o' time. Half hour at least." Maudie scrutinized her. "What else did you dream?" Pulling the almond milk from the fridge, Maudie ground some nutmeg to sprinkle on top of their chai.

"Then I was in a kitchen somewhere, lining cabinets and drawers with this big yellow floral pattern shelf paper. And I kept unpacking boxes—oh my God, so many boxes. But then as soon as I emptied a box, I had to move, so I repacked it. Then I'd be in another kitchen. It kept repeating—kitchen after kitchen. Except the shelf paper would be different patterns."

Maudie nodded. "So, in the dream, who said you had to move?"

Hannah strained to recall. "A man." She hesitated. "James."

"Mm. Interesting. You think it was the same James?"

"I don't know . . . maybe."

The coincidences were unnerving. There must be a logical explanation. Maybe reading the journal had caused that name to appear in her dream. She half hoped Maudie would jump in with words of wisdom. It was not the first dream Hannah had shared. It was, however, the first that felt so vibrantly real.

"Okay. Then what?"

"Then it shifted. I turned and saw this door like you'd see in a farmhouse—solid bottom and glass in the top. Kind of white, but the paint was chipped and peeling. It looked really old, unreliable. And on the other side, there was water, choppy waves under dark clouds, as if the house I was in was submerged. The water level kept rising and it was murky, but under the surface I could just barely make out . . ."

"What was there?"

"Books."

"On a shelf? Open? Closed?"

"Closed. Suspended. Being tossed around in the churning water. I was afraid."

"Of what?"

"That the door would break—and I would drown." She sipped her tea. "There might have been more, but I can't remember."

"Hmm." Maudie suddenly got up and opened a cabinet in the corner, returning with a medium size spiral bound notebook with a dark green cover.

"Here," she said, putting it on the table between them.

"What's that for?"

"For you to start a dream journal."

"A what?"

"A dream journal. Write down your dreams when you first wake up, 'fore you forget 'em. Might learn somethin' 'bout yourself."

"Ok, thanks." Perhaps her dream images could be helpful in her writing, even if they did nothing to help her remember.

Hannah set down her mug and her eye settled on "The Dreamer's Dream" on a bookshelf high up on the crowded wall. "What's that?"

Maudie turned to look. "Just some books I couldn't squeeze in on the shelves upstairs."

"I mean the dream one. What's that?" Hannah stood and reached up to inch it off the shelf.

"Don't remember that one. Phyllis must've left it behind." Hannah looked at her questioningly. "Woman friend who came for a visit some years ago. Psychic. Bit scattered."

"A psychic?" Hannah smirked and shook her head. "Seriously?"

"What? You don't think there are people who are psychic?"

"You do? I mean, come on." When she looked at Maudie, Hannah realized that she'd crossed a line.

"You best get going. Don't you have papers to deliver?" Maudie picked up the notebook she'd given Hannah. "Guess you won't be wanting that."

Hannah was taken aback. "I do. I mean—"

"You mean what? You think dreams actually might *mean* somethin'? Come on." Maudie dropped the notebook back on the table as punctuation and turned to wash her own mug.

"I'm sorry," she whispered. But Maudie was done with this conversation. Hannah waited until she left the kitchen to wash her own mug. To be helpful, she grabbed the sponge and wiped down the table, counter, and stove. She scrubbed at a stain, wishing she could wash away her snide remark.

Hannah glanced at the clock and pulled on the blue parka she'd gotten on sale at the thrift shop. Grabbing her helmet and biking gloves, she wrote "I'm sorry!" on a sticky note that she put on the table before stepping out into the cold morning air. She shifted her weight from one foot to the other to stretch before getting her bike from the garage.

She blew a puff of steam thick as cigarette smoke. *God, I wish I had a cigarette. Strange . . . I never smoked.* But a feeling of rejection rose to the surface like a dead fish, and with it the humiliation of feeling stinky. She had an urge to take a hot shower. She tried to hang onto the feeling—perhaps a memory—but it vanished as quickly as the steam.

She swung her leg over her bike and watched the second hand on her Micky Mouse watch tick forward a few seconds to 5:30. She pointed Ruby uphill. Pedaling for her life—perhaps toward some lighthouse in the fog, perhaps away from some darkness behind her. Both future and past crackled with static. Something deep inside reminded her it had not always been this way. Blur was not her normal state—she used to think clearly, knowing who she was and where she was headed. She must have had goals, a career, direction, hopes. That she was published confirmed she wasn't a total zero. She needed landmarks, some compass point for reference.

Riding provided at least a sensation of direction. As she pedaled, Hannah mentally gathered reassurances into an imaginary basket. It was Wednesday. The calendar with inspirational quotes on Maudie's wall had confirmed that fact. *That's comforting. Another fact: I got up at 4:45, if I can trust that old digital alarm.*

When Maudie first showed her the bedroom, she said the clock was two minutes fast. In her current hyper-awareness of all things misaligned, that was disconcerting. The idea that time could be ahead or behind—a specific time in the kitchen and two minutes later in the bedroom—made Hannah's life feel even more skewed. She assured herself that two minutes, in the larger scheme of things, was acceptably negotiable. And since it was the same clock each morning, it worked out somehow, despite the slippery quality of time everywhere else.

Fog brushed Hannah's cheeks. She was grateful she'd had hot tea as she leaned into the cold morning air toward the stack of papers awaiting delivery, Ruby's baskets rattling with anticipation. Paper delivery had been her first job as a kid, *The Sentinel* tossed onto porches in Bordentown. It got her out of the house—even better, it earned her money for books. She pictured kids riding their paper routes, weaving a web through neighborhoods like a fleet of little spiders. And she imagined people unfolding the papers in their driveways, waving to neighbors doing the same. *So Norman Rockwell. So Leave it to Beaver. So not my life.*

The traffic light at Park Presidio turned from amber to red before she reached the intersection. Hannah hit the brakes hard, grateful that the road was not as slick as usual. Crossing those six lanes without a solid green light was hazardous even at this hour.

She pulled out a handkerchief to wipe the drip forming on her nose. The light fog put a charming soft haze on all the lights. The morning felt ethereal, but Hannah's fingers were starting to numb as she waited. Impatient, she turned to take a different route, pedaling hard to heat her body, but the cold air cut all the harder into her fingers. She'd have to invest in warmer gloves: another trip to her favorite thrift store just off Lombard.

Hannah stopped, pulled the gloves off and rubbed her hands together. Blowing warm air into the gloves and the sensation of the warmth rebounding against her face pulled her like a tide into the experience of warming a little girl's mittens for her. As the

47

wave hit, she almost dropped her glove. *Oh my God, I do have a daughter!* What she had been unable to reconcile when reading the cookbook stories, she suddenly felt with absolute certainty, with solid conviction: This was fact. *The girl was about to board a bus . . . heading off on tour . . . a theater tour. Barely eight . . . too young to be entrusted to the care of a tutor and guardian, too young to travel the world performing. Too young for such a big dream. Why wasn't I going with her?*

Hannah dropped her bike, ripped open her backpack, and wrote in the journal the images that came to her.

The little girl was wearing a red coat with a woolly lining. Matching winter boots. Little nose and cheeks flushed with the brisk air and excitement. But I could see she was nervous. Her fingers were cold. Just like my mom had done for me, I took her mittens and warmed them with my breath. I told her, "I'm filling them up with love so it will be just like we're holding hands. That love will stick to you like bubble gum, even when you're not wearing your mittens. No matter what you do or where you go, my love will be right there with you." The girl put on the warm mittens and looked up at me with excitement and such tenderness that I wanted to cry.

"We'll be ok, Mommy. We'll both be ok. I'll write to you about my shows and everything." One more big hug and she turned to jump on the tour bus.

As the image faded, Hannah felt a shadow pull her from behind. She looked over her shoulder. The strip of park around her wept with the weight of the fog. Turning back to the journal she felt tears on her cheeks. Allie! *Allie is real.* Writing it brought even more certainty. How could she have forgotten—not believed—not *known*—that she had a daughter? She banged on the walls of the empty closet of her mind. *Where did they go? The memories of me and my child. How could I have lost them? I want them back!*

With the anguish came questions that spilled onto the page: *How old is Allie now?* She did the math: *Twenty-seven? Where is she? What happened to our relationship? Do we keep in touch?* She wrote with such ferocity the page started to tear. Then an earlier memory ran into her: *I was only eighteen. I was going to have an abortion—couldn't manage a kid alone. He was young, too—scared as I was. I was going to abort. But I must not have. But I remember it—so horrible—unforgettable—sucking life out of both the baby and me! Could I have imagined the nightmare of an abortion that vividly? Where is James? What happened to him? And what if Allie had never been born? What would my life have been—?*

Her pen stopped. Mind racing, she got up to pace the sidewalk. She had been in the hospital after the accident when they told her. "The baby is okay." The look on her face alerted the nurse to the fact that a baby was news. She couldn't call to mind whether James had been in the room at the time or not. But the decision had been agonizing, rending her with fears no matter whether she kept the baby or not. Would she be a terrible parent like her father, vacant like her mother? If she aborted, would she live to regret it? With a child to raise, would she have to give up writing—the passion she lived for that had made life endurable? What if she later wanted a child but couldn't have one? Hannah dropped to the ground, sobbing.

A car passed, slowing as the driver looked at her. She wiped her face and raised a smile, waved to indicate she was alright. *I have to call Allie—somehow I have to find her. What will I say to her? How can I explain it to her? What could I even tell her about my life? What could she tell me?*

A cold gust whipped at the journal, ripping the page from the binding and down the block. Terrified of losing this memory again, she kept her eyes glued to the paper as she threw her pack on and grabbed her bike to give chase. It stayed high enough to be out of reach, but she kept pace. As they neared the park, the wind swept it across Park Presidio. The light turned green just in time.

Hannah's mind twisted in the wind like the page, snatching at memories—determined to hold on to whatever she could find. *I remember meeting Maudie and eating cookies: my own Toasted*

Coconut Dreams. I'd been very hungry and ate more than I should have. Mom would have called me a pig—would sooner see me starve than risk anyone thinking she'd raised a daughter without the grace to go hungry when etiquette required the sacrifice.

But what had brought me to Maudie's in the first place? Memory was blockaded at that point. Access Denied. *I'd been out riding my bike. Where had I ridden from? Where was I riding to? What else have I forgotten?* An image of a mask covered with questions formed in her mind. Perhaps from a recent dream. *I'll have to write about it in my journal in case it means something.*

Fear climbed with her as she pumped up a steep hill, the journal page still pulling her forward. Maybe she did have some mental illness. Alzheimer's or dementia. Only forty-six, too young for that. But then maybe it would never feel that way from the inside. She felt like screaming. Her mother's voice insisted she pull herself together. *It's not acceptable to be out in public screaming like a maniac. I need to calm down and breathe. Maybe Mom was right about spending too much time in fictional worlds. I've been under a lot of stress recently, dislocated myself. That's probably it—stress is responsible for all kinds of terrible things—like memory loss.*

Her heart hammered, the cold air bit into her lungs. The climb steepened, but she downshifted too late. With gears grinding, she hopped off. The page caught on a pole across the street, allowing her to grab it. Relieved, she pushed it into her pack. Looking up, she found herself facing Ocean Breeze Meditation Center. A sign in its window read: "What are you grateful for?"

Her mind dropped into first gear. Everything around her went still.

What am I grateful for? She took a deep breath, slowly released it. *Grateful for Allie, wherever she is.* Further up the block she made out the shape of homeless bodies huddled in sleeping bags close to the buildings. *Grateful to not be sleeping on the street. For Maudie taking me in. For shelter each night. Enough food to eat. A warm jacket—well, sort of warm. Gloves, even these too-thin ones. For a job.*

Shoot, I've got papers to deliver! Hannah jogged her bike up the short steep section of the street before swinging her leg back over Ruby and riding on. *A good question to ask myself each day. I'll put a sticky note on the mirror.* The fog started to lift ever so slightly—both within and around her.

CHAPTER 6

Connections

JAMES

Night enveloped James when he exited his downtown office building in San Francisco, an icy gust confirming the arrival of the winter solstice. Two boys, caught up in their own world, bumped him on either side. Like a whirl of dry leaves, they darted around sparse clumps of holiday shoppers. Recovery was still slow four years after the banking crisis, and skinny Santas with bells and red buckets clung hopeful to the hems of stores, vying for loose change. James turned his collar up against the wind and a peppering of despair.

He skirted a woman trying to corral three boisterous kids. The smallest, holding a large lollipop behind her back, was defiantly backing away from her mother directly into his path. The mother glanced up at James, embarrassed, before catching her daughter's coat and sweeping her away.

Managing even a single child was daunting, as he had discovered while barely an adult himself. So painful, so blocked from memory that it had only recently resurfaced to remind him of his failure. All he knew was her name. He hadn't seen her since she was two. But now a recurring nightmare haunted him: a baby in a car seat—crying, but whenever he tried to approach, the car was further away. He shoved his bare hands into his pockets. A nerve near his left eye twitched.

The rains, which he'd expected to start in October or November, still had not arrived, though for several weekends in a row the heavens had threatened. As if to spite the drought in the Bay Area, the East Coast was digging out from relentless blizzards.

A small black terrier dragging a short leash trotted across his path, nearly tripping him. James stepped on the leash and the dog sat, looked up at him. "Where did you come from?" James frowned—no one was chasing it. He squatted to check the tag on the collar: *Toto*. He laughed. Toto yipped. "Well, Toto, looks like you're free to go, buddy. But in case you hadn't noticed, you're not in Kansas anymore." He scratched behind Toto's ears. "We might be in Oz, though, with those kids as munchkins from the Lollipop Guild." Toto tipped his head. "Go on." Toto trotted off toward a small crowd at the bus stop, then turned back to look at him.

A store security guard yelled, "Hey, you can't let your dog run like that. Leash law. You gotta hold the other end."

"Not my dog."

"Sure."

"What do you mean *sure*, I'm telling you—"

"I see what I see. Your dog followed you the whole block, even left a pile of shit that you didn't clean up by the trash can. And now you just let it run ahead."

"What? No, I . . ."

"If you can't be a responsible pet owner, you shouldn't be allowed to have one. Especially in the city."

James approached the guard, agitated. A woman in a tailored red coat dashed between them toward the store door. "Happy Holidays, Miss," the guard chimed, opening the door for her.

As the #80 bus pulled up, James followed the dog to the stop, glaring at him. Toto, unabashed, watched him board. James settled into a window seat near the rear door for the half hour ride. A young black man in a colorful head wrap slid in beside him. James was simmering.

"Bet that dude was surprised when you hopped on the bus

without your dog." The guy grinned.

"It wasn't . . ."

"I know, man, I saw the whole thing. He sure thought he had your number though. From his perspective you were guilty as charged."

"Well, his perspective was wrong."

The man shrugged. "Facts were wrong. His perspective was—just that. His. A point of view. Can't fault him for that."

"But he accused me wrongly!"

"Look around, man. People get accused of shit they didn't do all the time. Especially if they're wearing a different color skin. Some of us get a helping of that shit every day. Count yourself lucky."

James nodded. "Sorry. . . . Thanks."

The man nodded. "No worries, man." He settled in with earbuds, moving his head and fingers to the beat.

James gazed at the life of the city as the bus wormed its way through rush hour. They passed two men gesticulating, yelling at each other about what looked to be a minor accident. Onlookers kept their distance. *I guess every argument involves conflicting perspectives. Makes you wonder if there is any objective reality. Or are there only perspectives? Like the hawk and the lizard.*

He often rode into the city from the Park and Ride at Larkspur Landing. That way he could easily grab a bite at Marin Brewing Company, then cross the street to the movie house if he needed a respite from reality. He pulled out his own earbuds to search for trailers. While they loaded, he watched pedestrians moving quickly, sandwiched between physical reality and the reflection of the bus in storefront windows.

"Was a cute little fella, gotta admit," his seatmate commented.

"No sign of Dorothy or the Scarecrow though," James smiled at him.

"I get you, man. Like in *The Wiz*. Can't win—can't get outta the game. "

"So true," James shook his head.

"Time to change the tune, man." He started singing the chorus from "Ease on Down the Road," quietly, but with feeling.

James joined in. Some nearby passengers moved toward the door. The man's eyes had the same shape as Cal's. Their laughter triggered a memory of singing the same phrase with Cal as they'd goofed off one late summer night after seeing the film together.

The bus doors hissed open. A woman clenching a young boy's hand navigated through the crowd at the bus stop. They were well-dressed, but the boy's face was twisted with anger. "Juvenile delinquent, the early days," James joked, then realized that he'd just done to the kid what the guard had done to him. He turned to the young man beside him to comment, but his eyes were closed.

The bus pulled past a homeless man in a dirty sleeping bag with a black beanie, head bowed with exhaustion. His cardboard sign read *god bless you*—"god" not capitalized. The warm memory of laughing with Cal heated into a burning ache. *Don't you carry nothin' that might be a load,* he hummed.

He watched the trailers on his phone, leaning back in his seat. The action flick would be the best anesthetic. Resolved, he clicked over to blues by Delta Rae, volume low, and closed his eyes against the grating world of rush hour.

The bus crept along Lombard Street. A sudden swerve to the left startled him. The driver had given extra berth to a cyclist on a red bike with side baskets. Her reddish gold hair was tucked under a helmet. She looked up, annoyed. He caught his breath then felt for his backpack. Reassured he hadn't left it behind—his water bottle in the side pouch—he let himself drift back into the rhythmic music, vague memories of dancing with a woman with long, reddish gold hair and beautiful skin.

Shortly before his stop, he checked email. Instead of the work-related message he'd been eager for, he found one from Sam Olioli, his college buddy. James had last seen Sammo at Cal's memorial service, but they'd kept in touch, if once a year counted.

He'd emailed out of the blue about some book—*The Bond* by Lynne McTaggart. *James Bond, if I know Sammo. Odd to hear from Sammo about a book—he'd always been more into sports.* Signed "Sawubona," followed by a P.S.: *Sawubona* means *we* see you. It's a Zulu greeting that expresses the belief that each person is connected to all living things and the whole of consciousness.

James was disinclined toward the notion of being one with the obese woman with bad skin across the aisle. Ditto the shabbily dressed guy two rows up. And the one in the back mouthing off about being so lucky that he was out of jail that he'd kiss his attorney who got him off last time but he's got another court date next week and his car is impounded for driving with a suspended license and on he blathered. Even with the crap in his own life, he preferred it to what he was seeing around him. James hadn't noticed when his seatmate departed. *Maybe he was Cal's ghost.* He grinned at the notion and hummed the tune from *The Wiz* again.

At Larkspur Landing, he fought his way off the bus along with several commuters, snagging his sport coat pocket on something. The guy holding it was oblivious as James hurriedly wrestled himself free. The brisk walk to the restaurant was a relief, but it was crowded and noisy. *Now I'll have to rush dinner and miss the previews.*

"Sir?" The waiter led James to a small table and handed him a menu. "Today's specials include . . ."

"I'll have a small pizza with mushrooms and green onions. And any amber on tap. I'm in a hurry, catching a movie."

"Got it. Back faster than Wily Coyote."

James checked his email—still no response on the contract he was trying to fill. He set his phone on the table, wolfed dinner, dropped some bills under the empty plate, and dashed out.

The brew had taken the edge off his day, and the wind now shaved off the hint of sluggishness. Skipping the temptations of candy and popcorn, he sank into a seat in his favorite part of the theater—center rear—just as the lights dimmed. Perfect timing—again. Though he didn't note it—again. Slouching down, he let go of his day, inviting the images on screen to fill his mind.

The previews began with the trailer he'd watched on the bus. Odd, since previews were usually for films you hadn't already bought a ticket for. But he was here to escape the smog of his mind, so he didn't care that it wasn't the film he'd expected. Then the visuals of *Avatar* carried him into its rich, enticing world.

James had seen it before, loved the animation and effects and the great battle scenes, but this time it was the native community of Na'vi and their connection to the Home Tree, the Tree of Souls, the animals, and each other that held him. There was still a food chain and factions of peoples that didn't get along, but the underlying connection among them was palpable. His yearning grew strong enough to rise to consciousness—a longing for such community and connection.

Moving so frequently, he'd given up on maintaining friendships for the most part. Work had him on the phone and email most of the day, developing relationships that he maintained only within that context. At the end of the day, the last thing he felt like doing was calling anyone. Somewhere along the line he'd stopped making the effort to stay connected with friends. Easier to default to losing himself in a film.

He looked around the theater. The audience had clustered near the center, arms draped around shoulders and hands in shared boxes of popcorn. Teens elbowed each other and aimed popcorn into each other's mouths. Noticing made him feel even more alone. Sitting near the back let him exit quickly but cost him potential interaction with strangers. What he'd long considered a benefit, he now felt as a loss. The problem seemed to be compounded by the fact that he felt as lonely being in groups as he did alone—maybe even more so. There seemed no way to win.

His happiness felt shallow and short-lived, as if written in water on a blackboard of loneliness and grief.

Cal again—that turning point in his life had colored every-thing since. *Why? Why let that piece of the past block all future hap-piness? Other people seem to move on.* When he examined his pain objectively, it was less keen, and the guilt he carried like a pebble in his shoe less intense.

When the lights came up, James wiped his cheeks. Instead of rushing to beat the crowd, he waited until it was at its fullest to join the slow press. He shared a nod and smile with a young man and his date. As he stepped into the aisle, a man in a dark jacket with salt and pepper hair looked at him.

"James?"

"Phil?" The fact that he knew Phil's name surprised James. His impression was that they had worked together at some point, though nothing specific came to mind.

"Great film, huh?" Phil's smile was infectious.

"Yeah."

"You by yourself?"

James looked around. Phil laughed. "You look like you're not sure. Women don't appreciate being left behind. Hey, want to grab a beer? Been ages since I last saw you."

The film had shaken James up—perhaps in a good way. Good to have someone to process it with. "Sure, Marin Brewing?"

"Let's go."

They walked through the parking lot in silence, weaving through the headlights and across the four-lane street.

The clatter and chatter of the busy restaurant were welcoming, which surprised James. He noticed how each person shifted to allow them to pass. Rather than pressing past uncaring strangers, he actually felt part of the crowd. Young professionals who joked loudly—normally appearing self-absorbed and obnoxious—instead burbled with a warm buoyancy, raising his spirits.

"Table for two?" Phil asked the hostess.

"It'll be a few minutes, but we'll get you seated as soon as we can."

She turned away to respond to another customer.

James cursed—but Phil looked unbothered—even pleased.

As she turned back, apologizing, Phil smiled. "No problem." Within seconds a table for two opened. "Nice timing, huh?"

The same waiter who served James at dinner approached. "Welcome back. What can I get for you?"

While waiting for their beers, James reached into his coat pocket to see if that email had come in yet. "Damn it. My phone."

"You lose it?"

"Pocket's torn. Some idiot on the bus had a stick and my coat caught on it as I was getting off. My cell must've fallen out at the theater. Damn it."

"Hey, relax, they're open 'til midnight. We can swing by after we catch up."

"Yeah, okay, sorry." Phil's calm made it easier to settle down again.

Though James was here just a couple hours ago, he barely recognized the place. "That kid was my waiter at dinner. Different section. Huh. Funny coincidence."

"I've stopped believing in coincidences."

Thrown off by Phil's comment, James replied, "He's probably just covering a bigger area than I expected."

"Maybe. We can ask when he gets back." That struck James as a bit odd, but he brushed it aside. "So, fill me in. You still with CRG?"

"Yeah, still kicking around the country like a soccer ball in play. You?"

"Married, kid at home, and still with Fireman's Fund," Phil said.

"You look happy."

"I am. What about you?"

James just nodded. "You know, it's funny, I thought I was getting a ticket for a different film—some action flick that looked a lot less heady than *Avatar*. I've seen it before, but . . . wow, it hit me differently this time."

"It was a special showing. But I know what you mean. I've been doing classes at IONS, and it's blowing my mind, how interconnected everything is."

"IONS?"

"Ah," Phil smiled, "Are you a quantum newbie?" James was confused. "Institute of Noetic Sciences," Phil explained. "Quantum newbie is my own term. I take it you haven't been keeping up with the latest in frontier science."

James laughed, assuming this was a joke. "Never really been into science." Context was forming, allowing memories to bubble to the surface. "You were a sci-fi fan—or am I remembering wrong?"

"Yeah, but 'real life' is apparently more like science fiction than we ever guessed."

"How so?"

"Like we're all connected, one enormous sea of energy—just like in the movie." Phil's enthusiasm was contagious, even without James knowing what the hell he was talking about. Phil leaned back. "Sorry. My wife is always telling me to calm down." He leaned forward again with a big smile. "It's just SO cool."

The waiter returned and set their beers on the table. Phil asked his name, then said, "Thanks, Brett. So, my friend James says you waited on him at dinner but in a different section."

"Yeah, I was supposed to go home at eight, but one of the other wait staff called in stranded with a flat tire so we swapped shifts. It was lucky, actually, because my dad really needs my help tomorrow, but I'd been scheduled to work. So it's perfect. Oh, and . . ." He pulled a cell phone from his pocket and handed it to James. "You left this at your table earlier. I didn't expect to see you again tonight. Lucky."

"Thanks." James looked stunned. Phil grinned as Brett moved on.

"That was no coincidence. *That* was synchronicity in action."

"How is synchronicity different from coincidence?"

"Synchronicity is recognizing that things are happening in a purposeful, intentional, connected way. Coincidence is random."

"You mean like Brett's dad needing him and everything working out for him?"

"Yeah, and meanwhile a waitress may either want a day off or maybe just expects random problems—which invites it to manifest."

"Okay . . ." James was getting a little uncomfortable.

"You probably needed your phone back, but would you have come back if we hadn't run into each other?"

"No."

"You weren't even sure where you lost it—but things were organizing themselves to get it back to you."

James interrupted him. "That seems like a leap. I mean, sure, sometimes things work out, whatever. So—what—you're saying God or something is making everyone's wish come true on some cosmic chess board?"

Phil sat back again. "I use the word Universe to describe this conscious energy that we're all a part of. The word God—for me, anyway—sounds like some entity that sits in judgment or needs to be worshipped."

"Conscious energy? Come on."

"We're all making stuff happen. It's all good. And in a way, it's all God."

James thought Phil had flipped. Still, it was nice to hang out with a friend—even a nutty one. "Not sure what you mean exactly. Sort of sounds like you're saying we're all creating together. I kind of get that. But wouldn't that also mean that we all cancel each other out? Sort of randomize everything again after all? Besides, bad stuff is happening all the time when people don't want it to." James started thinking about Cal. Where was the good in that? His leg started to jitter.

"Of course. And when I say, 'it's all good,' I don't really mean that everything we're creating is stuff we would call good—we're creating what we focus on. Like the more we watch media coverage of war and stuff and feel crappy about it, the more we're creating it. We have more control than we think we do—more creative power. We're not separate like we've always been led to believe. And we're not victims of an objective, fixed world outside of ourselves that—"

"So, when one asshole shoots and kills someone else—what? He's just shot himself?" James closed his eyes and drank down his beer, wanting to numb the pain in his gut.

Phil became still, watching him. He slowed his breathing. Gradually, without noticing, James's breath slowed as well. "What happened?"

James, surprised by his emotional dive, felt his anger start to calm as his breath slowed. "My brother Cal. He . . . he was killed. Four years ago." James stared into his empty beer glass.

"I'm so sorry." Phil kept his eyes steady, but James could not bring himself to face his friend.

"It was stupid. Never should have happened. He was pissed at me over some stupid comment I made. Went off all mad and then pissed off some asshole with a gun who was on parole and . . . and the rest, as they say, is history." He saw Brett nearby and waved his empty glass. The waiter nodded.

After a long pause, Phil said, "Anger does that, doesn't it? It's very—attractive."

James looked at him suddenly, upset at his choice of words. "Attractive?! What the fuck—"

"I mean—magnetic. Anger attracts. Brings more anger to it. You know how it is when one guy is mad, it makes other people around him mad. That's all I meant. Anger breeds anger. Just like you said."

James began running down the familiar emotional path he'd travelled so many times. But hesitated. His haze was clearing into a different option. People usually commiserated with him, feeding his self-pity, raging at the world with him. He wasn't sure if he should be mad at Phil, but for the first time he could remember, the room didn't go dark with his anger and grief. There was a stillness like a blanket around him, buffering out the busy restaurant.

"That Tree of Souls in *Avatar* must have been powerful for you," Phil ventured. "Were you thinking about Cal then?"

James's chest rose with a swell of emotion. He felt it physically, but he'd trained himself to keep a lid on this. Yet the rising wave came so close to the surface that he dared not speak. His eyes had locked onto Phil's, though he wasn't seeing him anymore. He became aware of his fists on the table and then a gentle pressure on one of them.

He was relieved to not be alone. They breathed together until the wave receded.

The conversation turned then to easier topics—work and weather. When dinner was done, they said goodbye at the door. James picked up his car at the Park and Ride and headed home. In spite of the beers, he felt more awake than usual. He started to brake at the exit ramp light in central San Rafael, but it turned green. That was rare. All the rest of the way home, moving steadily down Third Street, he seemed to be hitting the lights perfectly. He really didn't feel like being home alone, so he backtracked to one of his favorite restaurants that had a low-key bar.

His mind paced back and forth along the conversation with Phil. He recalled the email from Sammo and thought about how Phil might describe the synchronicity.

His cell phone rang. It was late. *What's urgent at this hour?* James fished it out. "Sammo, what the hell?"

"I didn't wake you, did I?"

"No, but I was just thinking about you. It's like you were reading my mind or something. You guys are starting to freak me out."

"Oh, yeah? Me and who else?"

"Guy I used to work with: Phil. Talking about synchronicity

and the Universe with a capital U and stuff. I got your email. How the hell are you?"

"Good, really good. I was just thinking about you, too. Figured we hadn't talked in a while. Cool, yeah? Just like in the book. Did you pick it up yet?"

"You just emailed me a few hours ago. I've been at the movies—watching *Avatar*."

"Yeah? That's still playing out there?"

"Apparently I walked into the wrong theater and that's what was playing. Special showing."

"Yeah, or maybe you walked into the right theater."

"I'd seen it when it first came out, but it was like a different movie this time."

"Like how?"

"Not like they had changed it, but I saw different stuff in it. Phil was there. Hadn't seen him in years. We went out after and . . . and it came up about Cal . . . what happened. I've been so pissed off . . . I can't let go."

"I know, man."

"It's like a rash that itches like crazy but if you scratch it, it only gets worse. I fucked up. I just keep fucking up. I'm pissed at myself, I'm pissed at Cal . . ." James stopped to try to regain control of his breathing.

"You're doing it to yourself, man. It happened, sure. How you live with it is totally up to you, yeah? You choose your response."

"I've been trying to suppress my anger, but— "

"Fuck that! That's not what I'm talking about. Suppressing it is still being angry. What would it be like to *stop* being angry and just—I don't know—focus on how fun it was being his big bro for all those years?"

In the long silence, James's breathing slowed. He whispered, "I don't know."

"Maybe give it a shot, yeah?"

"Yeah," James breathed. "Yeah, okay."

"Okay."

"Wait, why did you call?"

"I was just thinking about you, man. I'll call you next week, yeah?"

"That would be great. Thanks, Sammo. You're a good friend."

There was a lump in his throat. But this one hurt in a good way.

CHAPTER 7

Tea Tags

HANNAH

When rain threatened, the papers had to be put in plastic sleeves. Today, storm clouds were blowing in from the ocean. Hannah would be lucky to get through her route before they hit. She pedaled up the hill as fast as possible.

Most were already delivered when the storm broke. Hail pounded her helmet. At a street corner she looked for shelter.

A woman in a thick bathrobe stood on the porch of the corner house. It was one of her customers. They had waved to each other a few times as Hannah had tossed her the paper. "Come on up!" she called. Hannah didn't stop to think, just ran through the hail and lifted her bike up the steps.

"Not really biking weather," the dark-haired woman smiled. Her voice was smooth as buttercream frosting.

Hannah shook hail off her helmet and grabbed a paper. "Neither snow nor rain nor heat nor gloom of night stays these couriers from the swift completion of their appointed rounds. Nor hail—they left that out. Your paper."

"Postal workers have trucks now."

"Sad but true."

"Paper delivery too, for that matter."

"I don't drive, so not an option."

"Above and beyond deserves a tip. Doesn't look like it is going to let up for a while. Come in for tea?" She looked sideways at Hannah as if uncertain the invitation would be accepted.

"Uh . . . okay. Sure, thanks." Hannah propped her bike behind a couple of chairs, figuring bike thieves would probably be under cover too. She followed the woman into a sitting room with a gas fireplace already lit.

"Have a seat. Herbal or black?"

Hannah sat on an upholstered chair, blue with a pattern of small yellow flowers, at a small round table in front of the fire. "Herbal, I guess."

The woman returned with three boxes to choose from. "Here you go. I'm Jaz." She extended her hand.

Hannah shook it. "I know. I mean, ah, you're a customer so . . . sorry, um, thanks for being a loyal subscriber. I'm Hannah."

"Hannah, which flavor?"

"Lemon Ginger, please. Thank you."

"Thank you for being such a dedicated delivery person." Jaz sat across the table from her. "Water will be hot soon. I've had my eye on you."

"Really?"

"Not in a creepy way, don't worry. There's not a lot going on out there at 5:55 each morning. You are amazingly consistent. Even in this weather. I'm impressed. Don't you ever sleep in or miss your alarm or—or have a flat tire?"

"Not yet, but it's only been a few months. Give me time." Hannah smiled wryly. "What gets you out of bed so early every day?" The kettle whistled from the kitchen.

"Meditation and yoga," Jaz replied over her shoulder. "But I have to wake up first, so I start with tea and the paper." She set a mug of hot water in front of Hannah.

Hannah sniffed the bag before dropping it into the water. "Mm. Makes me think of my grandmother—the scent of ginger candy on her warm breath. She loved ginger everything: tea, candy, you name it."

"Loved. Past tense."

Hannah slowly swished her teabag back and forth. "Yeah. I miss her. *And* our tea parties with ginger tea and oatmeal raisin cookies."

"Nice combo. She clearly had good taste. Homemade?"

"Is there any other kind?"

Jaz smiled and stirred honey into her tea. "Sounds like you were close?"

"Yeah. I lived with her about a year. Cancer got her in the end."

"I'm sorry."

"She'd been terrified of it—talked about it a lot—like she knew it was coming for her. It pounced on her like it sensed her fear and hunted her down. I was just twenty-one, and the helplessness in her eyes frightened me as much as the cancer had frightened Grandma."

Jaz nodded. "What we focus on expands."

Hannah felt affronted. "What's that supposed to mean?"

Jaz held up the tag on her tea bag. "I was just reading. Didn't mean to offend you."

"Oh." An awkward pause sat down between them. "I thought . . . nothing."

Jaz slowly dunked her bag, as the scent of peppermint and ginger cocooned them. "Do you believe that?"

"What?"

"That what we focus on expands. Law of Attraction."

"I'm sorry," Hannah sipped her tea, withdrawing, reprimanding herself for letting her guard down with a stranger. "I don't really get what you're talking about."

"Fear is powerful. Fear of cancer . . . fear of anything. But then, so is joy."

"What do you mean 'powerful'? Powerful how?"

"I was at the grocery store the other day and there was this long line at each register. And I noticed how the one clerk—the line

I was in—was cheerful and greeted each person with a smile and you could almost see it ripple right down the line, how her joy put a smile on everyone's faces. It made the wait feel inconsequential. And even though folks had lots of items, our line moved forward steadily. But the next line over the guy at the register seemed like a grump, like he was having a crap day. And you could see it ripple down his line. People were annoyed, checking the time, sighing and edgy. It was kind of amazing to witness."

"I don't think I ever notice stuff like that. Or maybe it doesn't happen around me." *Or maybe it was your imagination,* Hannah thought without voicing it.

"Have you ever heard of the RAS, the Reticular Activating System?"

"No, what's that?"

"Never mind. Just curious."

"Seems like if there's something to be upset about or happy about then it makes sense that everyone would just behave the way they're feeling, right?"

"Stimulus and response you mean."

"That's the way it works. I don't think there's anything mystical about it." Hannah had noticed that a lot of people in the Bay Area were into psychic, New Age stuff. Too woo-woo for her.

"Newtonian. A universe of tiny billiard balls."

"High school science class. Models of atoms."

Jaz laughed. "Okay. But what if the quantum physicists are right and we're actually more like wi-fi than billiard balls?"

"I have no idea. I was an English major—creative writing. Hard core science is way beyond me. I'm not smart enough for that stuff." She lifted her cup to her lips and held it there, guarding, as feelings of inadequacy started lining up to face her. She'd been enjoying the conversation, didn't like this shift.

There was something so . . . calm about Jaz, and so . . . present. Hannah had never met anyone quite like her.

"Where are you from?" Jaz asked. Hannah was discomfited

by the way Jaz' eyes seemed to see through her—her daily armor failing to protect her. She felt for a moment as if she'd neglected to properly close and bolt some door, that Jaz had quietly slipped into the gap with a flashlight and was now on the verge of discovering the internal mess.

She tried shutting that door. "What do you mean? Why do you ask that?" But clearly it was too late.

"I don't know—the question seemed to ask itself. You don't have to answer if it doesn't resonate."

The same question had been loitering around the edges of Hannah's mind, so that whenever she tried to reconstruct her recent past, it pelted her like the hail with further questions—such as why couldn't she remember, and had she lost her freakin' mind? She tried tiptoeing past the question. "I grew up in New Jersey."

Jaz just nodded, elbows resting on the table with her cup the keystone of a bridge, waiting for something more like an answer to the question that had walked into the room and now stood looming over them.

"I live in the Sunset district now." She paused, hoping it was enough. "Renting a room there." Jaz just sat, annoyingly still, disturbingly present. "Since October." Hannah inhaled the ginger aroma of her tea, hoping for some grandmotherly comfort and a reprieve.

Jaz set her mug down softly. "And what brought you to San Francisco in October?"

Direct hit.

Jaz seemed to recognize Hannah's fear. But instead of the expected twist of the knife, Jaz leaned back and looked out at the hail bouncing on the pavement outside, then glanced to the fire in the grate. The shift caught Hannah off guard. There was a kindness to it. She had braced for a defense or even the possibility of lashing out at Jaz for being nosey, but it was as if Jaz had made a martial arts move of no resistance.

Something else happened, too. Hannah found herself suddenly

wanting to spill her story—or lack thereof—to this woman she had just met. Very unlike Hannah, who had learned early on to keep her thoughts and feelings to herself. Expressing herself freely as a child was playing in a mine field. The small, pink diary with the tiny lock and key that she'd received for her seventh birthday had quickly become her best friend, locking away her deep interior in safety. Some sensation intimated to her that journaling had been a lifetime habit, filling once-blank books of all different sizes and bindings to overflowing. *Where are those journals now that I need them?* Hannah took a swallow of her tea. It was still hot enough to burn as it went down.

"It doesn't matter, you know," Jaz said. "Now is all that matters." She was so calm, so unaccountably, infuriatingly calm!

"How can you say the past doesn't matter!?" It was out. Hannah looked out at the hail to gather her thoughts, to try to pull herself together.

"I'm sorry, I—"

"I can't remember! I can't remember how I came to San Francisco. I can't remember where I came from. I can't remember huge chunks of my life—like most of my recent past. It's gone. I'm not even sure of who I am! How can I figure out who I am if I don't know who I was?!" She tried desperately to hold the tears back, but there was no stopping them now. A blunt silence followed. Hannah searched her pockets for a handkerchief. Jaz reached for a box of tissues and put it on the table.

Hannah stood up awkwardly and started to put her jacket on. "I'm sorry. I should go."

"You don't have to. It's okay."

"It's not okay. It sucks. Part of what makes it so frustrating is that it doesn't feel like it's just forgotten—it feels like it's gone missing—like something that was there is gone without a trace."

"I didn't mean to pry or upset you." Jaz reached out and put her hand on Hannah's arm. The hand was soft, and warm from holding the hot mug. "Hannah." Hannah stopped moving and let herself look into Jaz's gentle eyes. Tears blurred her vision. "Hannah, what we call our past, those things we call memories, they only matter if we let them. The only thing that truly means anything is right now. All of us forget far more than we remember anyway. What we choose to remember, we usually allow to shape what we are now—but that's a choice. I don't know why that question came up. Really, I didn't mean to upset you. Please forgive me."

"No, it's me. You didn't do anything wrong. I'm just an idiot sometimes," Hannah mumbled.

"You're not an idiot—you're a miracle."

Hannah looked at her like Jaz was possibly the crazy one, then forced an unbelieving smile. "You don't know me or you wouldn't say that." The figure of her father scowling with disgust stomped through her mind, calling out as it passed: *Shut your trap. You're pathetic.*

Jaz topped up Hannah's tea, then leaned back, retreating into her own thoughts. Hannah got the message and dropped back into her chair, wrapping her hands around the warm mug. The pattern of the wood grain in the table was like twisting worm trails. She began to follow one of the trails with her finger, getting lost in its maze. Her breathing slowed. When she looked up, Jaz was watching her with a gentle smile.

"I love this table," Jaz said quietly.

Hannah wondered at this woman. *If the tables had been turned, by now I would have been desperate to get this weirdo out of my house. But then, I probably never would've invited a total stranger into my house in the first place. Which one of us is the crazy one?*

"There's something—" Hannah began.

There was a long attentive pause. "What is it?"

"Don't take this the wrong way, but—there's something otherworldly about you."

"Cool! Thanks for noticing. I think there's something otherworldly about all of us. But most people are too stuck in this physical plane to notice."

This conversation was getting more alien by the minute. "I guess . . ." Hannah mumbled.

"Let me ask you this—who noticed?"

"Huh?"

"Who noticed I'm otherworldly?"

"Is that a trick question? I did."

"Okay. Who are you?"

"Yeah, I've been asking myself *that* question since I could think. And this recent memory-whatever-thing has only made things worse."

"So, if you don't have recent past to rely on, ruminate on, then it's like your life is a *tabula rasa.*"

"A what?"

"*Tabula rasa.* Clean slate. You get to start over fresh. Sounds like a gift."

"Doesn't feel like one."

"Yeah. But really, who are any of us?"

The image from a dream she'd had of a mask made of questions overlay Jaz's face. She twisted the tag of her teabag in her fingers. "I don't know. I mean, maybe I have a soul or spirit or something. I can think—sort of. Sometimes. Not so much right now. I have a mind, but that's just brain chemicals or something."

Jaz didn't let up. "Maybe. Ever observed your thinking?"

"Never had brain surgery. Especially not with me watching. That would be weird."

"You've heard of Deepak Chopra?"

"Sure, who hasn't?"

Jaz grinned. "Ever read anything by him?"

"Well . . . no."

"This is what he suggests: ask yourself what your next thought will be, then listen and watch for the answer."

Hannah gave a half smile. "Are you going all Yogi teabag on me?" Jaz looked perplexed. Hannah flipped up the tag on her teabag so Jaz could read it: "Observe yourself." They both broke into laughter.

"Synchronicity, gotta love it!" Jaz exclaimed. She topped up her own cup, so Hannah knew she was committed to stick this conversation out—no matter where it led. "So," Jaz resumed, "let's try it. Just for fun. Okay?"

"Okay," Hannah agreed, but she questioned whether it would be fun.

"Observe your next thought."

Baffled but willing this time, Hannah thought, *what will my next thought be?* then closed her eyes to avoid Jaz' unnervingly calm gaze. Hannah's mind swarmed with verminous thoughts, fretting about people discovering the secret of her missing timeline, worries about Allie and if she would ever find her, fears for her sanity. She opened her eyes to Jaz' deep brown ones watching her expectantly. Hannah looked down and swirled her teabag.

"I didn't think anything," she lied.

"Oooo, nice. Who was watching?"

"You were."

"That's not what I mean. Who in you was watching—observing? Noticing that you didn't think anything."

Her father's interrogating glare crept in, expecting answers she didn't have. "Sorry, I don't get what you mean." Her stomach revisited her college philosophy class—the teacher waiting for an answer to a question that sounded like it should be easy, but which eluded her under his fatherly gaze—her own father's, not Father Christmas's. She wanted to disappear, but the only thing coming to her was a growing sense of failure.

Tears pushed their way out, dripping down her face and onto the light blue cloth napkin, dark spots declaring her humiliation and failure.

"Hey." Jaz reached across the table and put her hand on Hannah's arm.

"I don't have any answers."

"You don't have to. I'm sorry. I just wanted you to experience your own consciousness. There is no known answer as to who that observer is—lots of scientists still trying to figure it out, but no answers."

Hannah looked up, miffed. "It was a trick question?"

"No, Hannah, it was just a question. Just trying to help you experience your own otherworldliness." Jaz got up from the table. "I should have made muffins or something." She started opening cabinets as if looking for food, without any clear commitment to finding any. Hannah felt for the first time that Jaz was perhaps as much at a loss as she was. She felt a twinge of responsibility for her host's discomfort. Hannah wished there was a relationship map to follow. She was lost. Floundering in unknown territory.

Jaz stopped rummaging. Quiet prevailed. They both looked out the window. The hail had stopped—her opportunity to escape. Hannah downed a final swallow of tea. "Thank you. I'm sorry I got all weird. I need to finish my paper route."

Jaz turned, looking concerned. "I'm sorry, too. I was just trying to help. We're all on a journey. I'm glad ours intersected."

"Me, too," Hannah said, though with less confidence than her new friend. *New friend—more likely lost customer. She'll probably cancel the paper after this disaster.*

Jaz walked with her toward the door. "Tomorrow?"

Hannah was taken completely by surprise. "What?"

"Tea tomorrow? Even if it isn't hailing?" She actually looked hopeful that Hannah would say yes.

"Are you sure?"

"Absolutely. I'll make muffins."

"I like muffins."

"Banana walnut okay?"

"Ever tried them with a bit of shaved toasted coconut?"

Jaz tilted her head and smiled. "Not yet. Sounds good though. 5:55 then?"

"Let's make it 6:02. You're near the end of my route, so I'll finish and circle back."

Jaz laughed. "6:02 then. Ride safely."

Hannah lifted her bike off the porch and navigated her way along the slippery streets. When she arrived home, she found a sticky note affixed to a box of ginger Yogi tea. "Saw this at the store and thought of you. Home later. Let's make some oatmeal raisin cookies! Sweeten things up."

Hannah smiled.

CHAPTER 8

Boxes

JAMES

James and Sammo sat in the living room in San Rafael, stomachs full from dessert, coffee in hand. James bathed in the warmth of his broad Samoan smile.

"You're crazy as a loon to come all this way to help me pack a few boxes, you know. I move all the time, it's no big deal."

"I know. But I wanted to catch you before you left this coast. Save me some miles. It's a holiday gift to myself. And no crazier than you are to keep moving so much. You barely got to the Left Coast and now you're leaving again."

"It works for me. I get restless. And—benefit of moving frequently—less baggage."

Sammo snorted.

"What?"

"You have more baggage than anyone I know."

"Don't be a smart ass or I may have to send you home."

They sipped in amiable silence.

James sighed. "Do you ever feel like your. . . ?"

"What?"

"Like your past is a blur?"

"Sure. Doesn't everyone? I went on this date about a month ago and we had a great time and we laughed and I'm thinking it was fun and we should do it again, yeah? So, I call her up a week later and she acts like it was a crap date, no fun at all, even denied that we had any laughs. Two people, same date, totally different memories of it. Makes you wonder about history books, yeah?"

"Yeah . . . well, I suppose we should get to it. Getting late." They set down their drinks and headed down the hall.

The green leaf pattern of the bedspread was buried under piles of clothes and a suitcase packed with things James would need over the first week in his new digs. In the open carry-on were toiletries, some clothes, and the book he'd bought yesterday.

Sammo noticed it. "You got it!"

"Hadn't planned to."

"Course not, cause you're a stubborn ass."

James smiled in spite of himself. "I was out last weekend, figured I'd take one final Bay Area bike ride. Gorgeous day. And I ride right past the San Rafael Library on my way home—it's just down the hill. Friends of the Library was having its sale on the lawn. Figured I'd take a look, maybe pick up a read for the flight. Walked up and it was the first thing I saw, on top of a stack at the first table I came to—like it was waiting for me."

"Love that."

"Maybe you do. I find it, frankly, a little creepy. Like someone's stalking me on a cosmic level." James picked it up and flipped to a random page. "'With every breath we take, we are cocreating our world.' That's a scary thought. The world's fucked up. Why would we create stuff we clearly don't want? You should take it with you and give it to someone who wants to turn their back on reality."

Sammo didn't take it from him, and James tossed it back on the bed.

"I thought that was exactly what you wanted. A different reality."

"Okay, yes, a different reality, but still reality. Not some wishful thinking, parallel universe, Avatar land." James handed Sammo a cardboard box. "Here, you can pack clothes."

"Everything?"

"Leave me one pair of pants and three shirts, boxers, socks, you know."

"Got it." He grabbed a bunch of shirts from the closet and dumped them on the bed to start folding.

James started emptying the dresser. "If I'm going to live in a parallel universe, I want it to be one in which Cal is still alive."

Sammo stopped and, picking up the book to make room, sat on the bed. "But if there were one of those, then wouldn't there still be a version of you in this one? Without Cal?"

James sat next him, considering this. "I guess so. Are you saying you think there is such a universe?"

"Beats me. But maybe. Seems like we'd never know even if there was."

"Feels better somehow, thinking that there might be. There was this woman at the sale, I don't know, sixties maybe. And she sees me holding the book and she says she read some other book by the same author or something like that and it changed her life."

"Did you ask how?"

"She said it helped her stop being angry."

"Yeah?"

"Yeah. Said 'We have more control than most of us give ourselves credit for,' something like that. That she stopped blaming and started taking responsibility for her life and that's what made the anger lose its grip. Then she's like 'Or maybe it just split me off into a parallel universe. Who knows? Anything is possible.'" James snorted. "Is it? Anyway, I bought the book." Sammo held it up for him to take. "Okay, okay, I'll read it."

"Cool." They went back to packing. "Where on the East Coast did you say you're going?"

"Princeton, New Jersey. Back to my home state. Further south than where I grew up though."

As James packed, he quietly counted aloud as if doing an inventory.

Sammo laughed. "You still do that thing."

"What thing?"

"Counting. You count everything. It's a wonder you're not a CPA or something. A bean counter."

"Can't help it. When Cal was learning to count, I counted everything out loud to help him learn. Made our parents happy, proud of what a good big brother I was. I wasn't though. I was a jerk. Made me feel superior—especially when I got to the higher numbers Cal hadn't learned yet."

"You don't give yourself much credit."

"Credit for what? Being a failure of a brother?"

"No, for being a brother who was also a kid growing up. That's what big brothers do. My brothers used to sit on me 'til I would stop squirming and they thought maybe they'd squeezed the life out of me. Or they'd tie me to a tree 'til Mom called us to dinner. That's just being brothers."

"Yeah, well, Cal was . . . different, you know . . . not like you and me . . . he had . . . special needs."

"He was still your brother. And you were still a kid. And I'm sure he knew you loved him. So cut yourself some slack."

"I think we're done in here. I'll hit the kitchen if you want to do the bathroom. Leave out my toothbrush and toothpaste." Sammo picked up an empty box from the hallway.

James loaded up kitchen ware: skillet, hotpot, blender. He was disconnected from it all, didn't even remember unpacking the stuff just two and a half months ago. Mostly he ate out, but he packed two table settings—twice what he could possibly need, which felt excessive, but he was covered if he mangled a fork in the disposal. He never had anyone over—though Sammo's visit was a rare and unexpected exception—and he washed up after every meal.

Most of the stuff lying around the house didn't qualify for a box. *How did all this junk accumulate? Pens everywhere!* The small closet by the bathroom produced a few more boxables: two bath towels, three hand towels, four washcloths. He added the queen size set of bedding, just in case.

As he did, Sammo came out of the bathroom. "What's this?" He held out a thin silver necklace with charms that looked like little silver pencils and erasers. It looked vaguely familiar, so light that he could barely feel it.

"I don't know. Where did you find it?"

"I was emptying the medicine cabinet and a pair of tweezers dropped. I went to pick them up and saw it under the edge of the bathmat."

"Weird. It's not mine."

"From a date?"

"Haven't had any."

"Seriously? You used to go through relationships like you now go through job assignments. Always someone new, every time we talked."

"Really?"

Sammo looked at him with concern. "What's going on with you, James?"

"Nothing." He stuffed the necklace in his pocket. "I'll save it. It'll make a gift for someone. Let's do the living room, then call it quits. I'm beat."

There were few temptations in the living room. Just above a singed spot on the wooden mantle, in a handcrafted frame was his favorite photo: one of very few he had of the brothers—James at sixteen, smug and arrogant, and Cal at thirteen holding two fingers behind James's head, clearly pleased with himself. Cal had caught up to James in height by the time he was five and kept pace through the years, making it harder for James to protect him from bullies. Though Cal didn't know what "dimwit" or "ignoramus" meant—didn't realize he was being picked on—James couldn't tolerate it. His own teasing was brotherly, like puppy wrestling. Bullies were just mean.

James picked up a photo of his parents. "I went to the cemetery this morning, before you got here. Up in Sacramento."

"Where Cal's buried?"

"Cal and Mom."

"I thought you grew up in Jersey."

"I did. Mom moved out here with Cal when I started college. Mom's health had suffered after Dad's heart attack, but she held on—mostly for Cal. Her sister lived in Sacramento and Mom wanted to be closer. Seemed like a good idea. But then about six months later, Aunt Laurie died. Mom took it hard. A year later her broken heart just gave up—but not before making me promise to look after Cal. That's why I dropped out and left."

"So that was the family emergency."

"One of them."

He hadn't been to the gravesite in four years, not since Cal was laid in an adjacent plot. At Cal's burial, he'd been too ashamed to even look at his mother's grave. After placing a bouquet of daisies—Cal's favorite, and another of roses—the flower his mom was named after, James sat in the grass between them. "I'm sorry, Mom. I promised to take care of Cal, but I screwed up. Big time. I got mad and told him not to act so stupid. I shouldn't have said that."

He turned to Cal's grave. "You were right, Cal. *I* was the one who was stupid. When you took off, I figured we'd both cool off and you'd come back. But you didn't. Damn it, Cal—you were supposed to come back! I'm sorry, Mom, I was about to go hunt for him when that girl called—the girl who found him." James pulled out a handkerchief, furious he couldn't stop the tears or repair the damage he'd caused.

Shame and guilt weighed him down, and he'd left to go home and greet Sammo who was arriving from southern California.

James now wiped a thin layer of dust from the framed photo with his sleeve, then placed it carefully in the box.

A small envelope that must have been stuck to the back of the frame fell to the floor. It was blank and yellowed with age.

Sammo picked it up and handed it to James.

A shadow flitted by as he sat slowly, staring at it.

Inside was a photo of a curly-haired toddler in the arms of a woman with waves of golden hair. A deep sadness stirred within James, and he lost his mental balance, seeing his past from within a hall of mirrors, a kaleidoscopic jumble of memories, dreams, regrets, imagination.

Tears flowed as his mind ran desperately down one path then another, came to dead ends and loops, and endless reflections, but no exit. He felt a warm hand on his shoulder, pulling him back.

"Your kid?" Sammo asked quietly. James nodded, mute. "I didn't know. Is she . . . Where is she?"

James shook his head. "I don't know. I haven't seen her since she was about two. I screwed up—bad. And they left, they disappeared. I didn't try to find them. I . . . I came to California. Mom was dying. I'd just gotten the call and I—oh, man, I was a mess. All I could see was my life falling apart. I loved Cal. God, I loved him so much. But I also wanted a life of my own. I couldn't even tell my mom about the baby, I—I didn't want her to come back. I was trying to move on." His breathing became shallow and labored.

Sammo knelt and put a reassuring hand on his arm.

"It was an accident, we were careless, and we were going to abort, but . . . I thought about Dad and what he would tell me to do. 'One step after another, Jimmy. That's the only way to do it. One step. Then one more step.' So we had Allison. And that day—the day I got that call about Mom—I had just put Allison in her car seat to take her to the park. Hannah's grandmother had given us her car—mine was a piece of junk—since she couldn't drive anymore. And I . . ." James sucked air in gulps. "I drove off in the wrong car. I got to the park—it was only a few minutes away—but realized and raced back. But Hannah had gotten home on her bike and found her. She was furious, of course. And that was it. She said she couldn't trust me and didn't want her kid to grow up with a dad who cared as little about his kid as hers had."

"Oh, James . . ."

"She was right. So she left and I never tried to find them." He looked again at the photo.

"How old would she be now?"

"Twenty-six . . . twenty-seven, I guess."

"Maybe you should try to find her."

"Even if I could, what would I say? Hannah was smart to run away with her. I was stupid."

"You were young. And under a lot of stress, yeah? Your mom was dying. You were trying to start your life, but you had to take care of your brother."

"Yeah, well, I wasn't under much stress when I drove my brother off to get killed."

"You didn't know he was—"

"I was mean. Cal knew it. I knew it. And if I hadn't been such a jerk, he would still be alive."

"You don't know that." James looked at him, questioning. "That's a story you're telling yourself, but it's not helping you or anyone else."

James looked again at the photo. Freedom tugged at his sleeve. *Let it go. Come on, let it go. One step.* He tucked the photo into the box with the framed one of him and Cal.

"Let's take a break, yeah?"

"I need some air," James said. They stepped out onto the deck, the lights of San Rafael sparkling through the branches below.

"Seems like everywhere I turn, Cal shows up to face off with me. Cal loved beaches and hated coffee shops. So I avoid beaches and make sure to find a favorite cafe in every city I land in."

"You always have been an ornery SOB."

"Too cold out here. I'm beat. Let's call it a night."

A few items needed to be cleared from the bed before James could climb in.

What if . . . what if in a parallel universe we'd made a different decision about the baby? What would it be like there? Would Cal still be alive?

Good thing I'm getting out of the Bay Area. Giving me crazy ideas. He picked up the book he'd agreed to read. *Frontier science? More like frontier foolishness.* He stared at it. Flipping it over, one of the quotes grabbed his attention: "We all want a better world, a better life, but many people don't have the courage to take that first step."

"*Chicken! Bok, bok, bok!*" Cal taunted.

James tossed it into his carry-on bag. "Am not."

A missed shoebox in the closet caught his eye, and he pulled it out, looked through the few family photos he had. He laughed seeing himself at nine, Cal riding him like a horse, on all fours. Right after their mom snapped the picture, James had bucked him off—right into a fresh dog pile, raising a stink in every meaning of the word. The beautiful irony—it had been Cal's day to clean up after their mutt. And Jimmy got to hose Cal off in the yard. James laid it on top of one of their newlywed parents.

Tucked in with the photos was a home-sewn brown flannel bag. James pulled out the harmonica and rubbed his thumbs over the design etched on the side. Mom had still been in intensive care a week after her heart attack. He'd gone to her apartment for a respite from the bedside vigil. Cal stayed with her. Looking for something to cheer her up, he'd found this among random buttons, bits of ribbon, and bobby pins in her dresser.

Curious, since no one in the family played that he knew of, he'd brought it to the hospital. She was awake, Cal holding her limp hand. Her eyes lit up. "Daddy's harmonica."

"Grandpa played?"

"Oh yes. Beautifully. He called it Marie. 'Me an' Marie will sing for you, Rosey,' he'd say to me. Oh, the tunes he'd play! Sometimes I'd get up and dance. I always wished one of you boys would take it up." She smiled weakly. "Who knows? You're young yet. Maybe Marie will sing for me again one day." She looked hopeful.

"Sure, Mom," James said with as much enthusiasm as he could, as the light in her eyes dimmed, like a very slow fade-to-black at the end of a movie he did not want to end. "I'll give it a go." She smiled weakly.

Cal punched him lightly. "Just make sure I'm out of earshot while you're learning. Remember you trying to play the trumpet? Oh, man! You were bad, you were so bad."

"I wasn't *that* bad."

"You were so bad all the neighbors would clear out to the grocery store so's they wouldn't have to hear you." They laughed, then turned to see if Mom was laughing, too. But she'd slipped away as quietly as she'd slipped out of their bedroom after tucking them in.

James swallowed the lump in his throat and slowly brought it to his lips. He'd never blown into it. From city to city, box to box, James had carried it intending to keep his promise to his mom to try to learn to play. His lips touched the cool metal sides. *Just breathe.* His breath hesitated like a shy child, withdrawing into the shadows of his lungs, crouching and fearful. *Breathe.* His father's gentle voice coaching. *Breathe.* Finally, with a slow, sad sigh of release, the air flowed through his mouth into Marie.

He did not expect music, but her mournful sound surprised him, as if she had her own way of using the air given to her. James paused, then wrapped it in its cloth bag and put it gently in his suitcase. He and Marie would find a way to make music, to breathe together. It would take time, but he would keep this promise. *And I'll play well, Cal, just to prove that you were wrong—you, asshole!*

CHAPTER 9

Time Zones

HANNAH

"Hello?" The voice sounded familiar, maybe . . . and tired.

"Allie, is that you?" Hannah had rehearsed those four words over and over, simple and safe. The phone number Hannah had managed to dig up, after hours of online research, promised no guarantee of reaching the young woman she believed might be her daughter. Though Hannah realized there was still a possibility that she had manufactured the parting scene with her perhaps-imagined daughter as well as the daughter mentioned in her cookbook, she felt ninety percent certain of their reality.

"Mom? Oh my God. Are you okay? Is something wrong?"

"What? No, I'm fine . . . I—I was just thinking about you."

"Really? Okay. Are you sure everything is okay?"

Hannah swallowed. *No, I'm not sure everything is okay. In fact, I'm quite sure things are not okay at all. But this is not where I want to start this conversation with my long-lost (how long?) daughter. Trying to explain would most likely lead Allie to believe she had totally lost it. Definitely not the plan.* Hannah had imagined this call since that cold morning about three weeks ago warming her gloves. *"Sorry I haven't called—I forgot you existed."* Or *"I totally forgot I had a daughter, so not sure when we last spoke. How have you been?"*

Hannah twisted in her seat. It felt like the earth under her feet kept shifting, and not because she was living in earthquake territory. She hoped that reconnecting would ground her, give the seemingly random flashes of memory a safe landing place. Vivid dreams, day and night, felt increasingly like memories, but had not yet coalesced into a cohesive whole.

"Mom? You still there?"

"Yeah. What's up with you these days?" Hannah tried to sound light and easy, but sensed she wasn't succeeding.

"Well," Allie sounded tired, "we're still on the road with *Mama Mia*, but we're here in London for a while. It could run another year—that's the word in the green room. There was a big producer meeting last week, the house is full most nights. So it's good. London is brilliant. The Tube—that's the subway, you know . . ."

"I know."

"Yeah, so the Tube makes it easy to get wherever. Austin and I, well . . ."

"Austin?"

"Mom, don't make like I never told you—it's been over a year we've been together. I know we don't talk much, but—"

"No, it's the phone. The signal is weak. I thought you said something about Boston." Hannah bit her lip. Confirmed: they haven't talked frequently. Noted: Allie and Austin. Confirmed: Allie is in London—must be late there. "Gosh how long has it been since you landed in London? Seems like . . ."

"Six months. Crazy, huh? Time is insane."

"That's for sure. I guess we should be Skyping or something. I wasn't sure I'd get you."

"Generally that's better. But . . . maybe a bit earlier? It's one in the morning and I've got a matinee tomorrow."

"I'm sorry, Allie, I wasn't thinking about that. I was just remembering how I warmed up your mittens the day you left."

"Whoa. Throw back. You in menopause or something?"

"Probably."

Allie seemed to sense her mom's need to connect. She snuggled into her pillow with the phone. "Sometimes I'd even wear those mittens on hot days, because you'd filled them up with love."

"You remembered?" Hannah's voice was small.

"Oh yeah. Hey, do you remember that time we put Elmer's glue all over our palms, then blew on it to dry—and peeled it off like skin?" Allie heard the intake of breath, knowing she'd found a good one. "I used to make my tutors do that with me, telling them my mom said I had to. And I'd keep them for as long as I could. Thinking of you. Love you, Mom."

"Love you. You get some sleep. We'll catch up later."

"'Night, Mom."

"Good night." The phone went silent.

Hannah inhaled deeply and held in the air a few seconds. *I have a daughter! At least my mind isn't manufacturing false memories.* Looking out at the plum tree, she smiled. She grabbed her journal—the one from the apartment she'd visited.

Hannah had started adding to it to track memories, finally convinced that she was the author of that Prologue and Chapter One. It was in her handwriting. But she couldn't tell yet whether it was the start of a novel or a journal of her life. *If it's a journal, who is James and where did they live in Marin? It doesn't line up with the info about Bob or Allie or living in San Francisco.*

If she was suffering short-term memory loss since arriving at Maudie's, notes she was making in the journal should uncover patterns and something to go see someone about—doctor or therapist. Journaling was always a good idea for writers anyway. *Maybe someday I'll write about a woman who lost her mind. Hell, I could write that now.*

The door downstairs opened. Packages were plopped down, Maudie's boots shuffled on the wooden floor toward the kitchen then back to the hall. Closet door opened, coat hung up, an umbrella dropped on the floor. Rain had threatened. Maudie always went out prepared for whatever weather might show up. Packages were hoisted with a grunt and carried to the kitchen.

Maudie's muffled voice climbed the stairs. "Hannah? You home? I got the butter!" Refrigerator door, cabinets, drawer—so Maudie must have bought tea. "Hannah?"

"Up here! I'll be down in a couple minutes!" Hannah wanted to make sure she captured everything Allie had said during the call. The phone number also went into her journal with the date and time, in case she needed to corroborate it later.

Satisfied, she slid into fuzzy slippers she'd picked up on sale at a discount store on Clement Street. Brown and white with big sad puppy eyes. She recalled the conversation at the cash register. "Fifty percent off. Must be the eyes."

"Sorry?" Hannah loved the sad look on the puppy face.

"All the other ones look happy." The woman pointed to a rack of cheery puppy slippers looking eager to be purchased. "You still want these?"

"Yeah. I mean, I feel kind of sorry for them, you know? They look so sad."

The clerk smiled and rang up the purchase. "I'm sure you'll give them a good home."

"Dogs for my dogs." The clerk looked puzzled. "Feet."

"That'll be eight forty-five. Cash or credit?"

"Cash." Hannah dug in her pocket. "That's pretty cheap."

"Half off."

"Probably made by a half-starved, horrifically underpaid child laborer on an assembly line somewhere in a third world country."

The clerk looked at the tag. "China. Yeah, probably. You could pay more if you want, but it wouldn't make it to the kid." The clerk handed Hannah the slippers in a bag.

"Keep the bag. Least I can do is reduce waste. That won't help the kid either, but . . . it's something." She'd stuffed the slippers into her pack.

When Hannah had pulled the slippers out at home, she studied them. The assembly-line worker must have been having a bad day. She chided herself for spending as little as possible and supporting wretched labor abuses to keep her feet warm every morning—and for what having so little cash forced her to do when that kid went without. *Honestly, how can I consider myself anything but wealthy in comparison to that kid in China? Probably a skinny boy in rags with big brown eyes like the puppy. I've seen photos, lots of them. That kid exists, whether or not he had any connection to these slippers.* But Hannah's mind had connected the two. She imagined him squeezing a drop of glue, watching it ooze out and plop in place, then placing the eyes upside down and sending it on down the assembly line. *Maybe his mother working beside him put on the nose.*

Allie had gone off to be a child laborer of sorts—but by choice. Performing in a national theatre tour was certainly work. But it was also her dream, not driven by a desperate need to survive.

Since the slippers were made in China, she named the little boy Lee. *I promise to love the sad doggies because you made them, Lee. I appreciate your gift to me. Please forgive me.*

Allie said it was 1:00 a.m.—eight hours ahead of her. Hannah pictured her snuggled in bed. Lee was another eight hours ahead, on the assembly line probably—dreaming of the lunch he wouldn't have. Hannah and her kids, Allie and Lee, spanned the globe in equidistant time zones. Hannah had mentally adopted Lee—simpler and cheaper than physical adoption. But she would hold him in her heart whenever she wore these slippers. And maybe she would try to figure out a way to visit Allie.

A crash made Hannah jump to her feet. She sped downstairs, her steps muffled by her new slippers. Maudie was bent over, picking up pieces of a plate. "Are you okay?"

"There you are, Hannah. Lord, what a mess. I thought it might be fun to have tea and scones on this plate, but it was on the top shelf. It slipped."

"I'll clean it up." Hannah turned over the two largest pieces to find an old map of London—what a coincidence. She set them in the dustpan Maudie held for her. Something caught her eye on the bottom of one if the pieces. She examined the tiny gold label: "Made in China."

"Tea—and scones?" Hannah was sorting out the jigsaw puzzle of coincidences in her mind.

"What, don't go telling me you don't like scones. I bought blueberry." Maudie pulled two from a bakery bag. "And my favorite tea at the Asian grocery on the corner."

"I love scones. And tea." Hannah tipped the dustpan of ceramic pieces into the trash.

"Put the kettle on, girl." She frowned at the trash can. "Too bad about that plate. Oh well, it's just a thing. Just a thing." Maudie unpacked the rest of the groceries, then noticed Hannah's feet. "Those new?"

"What? Oh, yeah, got them today. Where did you get the plate?" Hannah asked.

Maudie plopped herself into one of the kitchen chairs after pulling two small blue plates from the cabinet. "James Frank— but he was Jimmy Frankie to me."

"James," Hannah murmured. But the thought attached to the name slipped away into Maudie's words.

"Jimmy had just started courtin' me—old fashioned term, but that's what my mama called it and I liked the sound better than datin'. Made it seem like more than just a boy chasing a girl. Anyway, he came by and we went walkin'. I figured out later that my mama musta liked him, 'cause she tipped him off it was my birthday. So we're walkin' along and he slips into this secondhand store—I didn't know what he was up to. I asked, but he just told me hold my horses and stop askin' so many questions. He comes out all Mr. Top Secret with a brown bag flat as a pancake. Then we come to this bakery next block an' he tells me to wait outside again while he goes in. Couple minutes later he comes out with a box, right? But he won't tell me anythin', and we get to the park and sit on a bench and he pulls out this chocolate cupcake on the plate and there's a candle in the top and even a fork. And napkins. He assured me that he had the bakery girl wash the plate before she put the cupcake on it. That little fact set him apart from the average boy. Jimmie Frankie was fine. Fine man. Good husband."

"He was your husband?" Hannah picked up the whistling kettle and filled the teapot. "I didn't know you'd been married."

"Two years. Mighty fine years they were, too."

Hesitantly Hannah asked, "What happened?"

"Woman in an SUV on 280. Pulled out right in front of him—didn't see him on his motorcycle. No way he could swerve around—slammed right into the back of her. Met his Maker on the bumper of a damn SUV."

"God, I'm so sorry, Maudie. You want me to try to glue that plate back together?"

"No. Jimmy and I had two fine years. Better than gettin' sick of each other over forty-two, don't you think?"

"I guess, yeah."

"You ever been married?" Maudie asked, dipping her scone into her tea.

Suddenly Hannah was wrestling with a ghost, trying to pin it down, to get a glimpse of it. She had managed so far to avoid talking about her past or confessing just how little of it she actually remembered.

Maudie swallowed and touched Hannah's arm. "I'm sorry, honey, I had no business asking. Just forget—"

"No," Hannah interrupted, "that's the problem. I don't want to forget. But I do forget. No matter how hard I try. I can't remember much of anything from before I came here. I remember some things. It's not like amnesia where I don't know who I am. It's more like I don't know who I was. It's hard to explain."

"I been wonderin' but didn't want to pry. Figured you'd tell me in your own good time. You think maybe something traumatic happened or somethin'? Like you blocked stuff out?"

"I had been thinking maybe it was something simple, like I'd just lost my freakin' mind." They both laughed.

"Most of us carry our yesterdays around like they're all we've got. But really, it's today that counts. Only place we have any agency to make our tomorrows better."

"Seems hard to know where I'm going if I don't know where I've been."

"That's jus' from focusin' on the rear-view mirror. No wonder so many of us end up in ruts or a ditch or jus' clear off the road altogether. Shift your attention left a bit and you can see out the windshield."

Hannah let that sink in.

"I have a daughter," she blurted.

"You do?"

"Yeah."

"Did you remember her right along? I have some friends who sure wish they could forget they have kids." They laughed again.

"Only since a few weeks ago. I was warming up my gloves, blowing warm air in—I wasn't even sure if it was a real memory at first."

"My mama used to do that for me. She told me it was a sight better use of her hot air than trying to get Daddy to take out the trash."

"I called her today," Hannah admitted with hushed excitement.

"Your daughter?"

Hannah nodded. "She's in London. On tour."

"What kind of tour? She in a band or somethin'?"

"Musical theater. She's been touring since she was eight. Her leaving was what I remembered."

"How old is she now?" Maudie asked.

"Twenty-seven."

"And she's been gone all that time?"

Hannah sighed. "Well, maybe not, I don't really know. It's so weird."

"You got any other kids tucked away somewhere, you s'pose?" Maudie looked concerned about who else might have been left behind.

"The only other kid I can think of is Lee, but he doesn't really count."

"Lord have mercy, now you're making me nervous. Who's Lee and why doesn't he count?"

Hannah laughed. "It's okay, it's an inside joke—like inside my head. He's the child laborer who made my slippers. I imagined him." Hannah lifted her foot high in the air to show Maudie. "Those eyes . . ."

"I see. But you're sure you didn't make up the daughter too?" Maudie asked cautiously.

"I wasn't sure until I called her and talked to her. Allie is real."

"Nice name."

"I was even thinking of trying to visit her. Maybe it would help me figure stuff out. But I don't know how I could ever afford it. I'd have to deliver a heck of a lot of papers!"

"Well, anythin' is possible. You want somethin', you set it in your mind and hatch it like an egg. Keep it warm. Pay attention to it. One way or another that chick will find its way out. But don't go messin' with it and tryin' to figure out how it will get out, or you might just crack the shell too soon and keep it from comin'. Dream on, girl! And I mean that. Nothin' happens without a dream happenin' first." Maudie smiled and poured another cup of tea. "I thought myself up a woman friend rentin' that room upstairs and look who showed up on my doorstep."

Hannah looked up at her. They both smiled.

CHAPTER 10

Surfing the Life Wave

JAMES

James, back at CRG, stared at his online bank balance: $11,111.11. He shook his head and logged out.

Is the world around me changing—or am I seeing it differently?

He pictured his friend Phil back in California, talking about synchronicity. The weirdness of that conversation had seeped into his life. Things he once perceived as random or coincidental looked more ordered and interrelated. More like a jigsaw puzzle than a set of billiard balls.

In college, his friend Bethany had liked to pretend she was psychic. Whenever the phone rang she announced the caller in a breathy voice as if she were reading a crystal ball, though the caller ID was obvious. It always made him laugh. *Whatever happened to her?*

The phone jolted him back into business mode. He didn't recognize the number. "CRG, this is James."

A breathy female voice said, "You'll never guess who this is."

He sat up straighter. "Sorry, I don't have your number programmed into my phone . . ."

"James, how could you not know who is calling?" She erupted in laughter.

"Is this—? What—? How did—?"

"It's Bethany! Remember? I've never heard you at a loss for

words, but if you tell me you forgot who I am, I'll diagnose you with Alzheimer's. I mean, come on, it hasn't been *that* long." She paused. "I don't think. Has it? How long's it been?"

James was struggling to regain his balance. "Years. How did you even get my number?"

"Don't be an idiot. It's the same one you had at school. I heard you move around a lot, but at least you've kept your phone number. Good boy."

"But—why are you calling? I mean . . ."

"Wow, you don't sound very pleased to hear from me."

"No, it's not that. I just—I mean, it's weird, I was just thinking about you when bam, the phone rings and—I just don't . . ."

"Cool. Nice to know you were thinking about me." Bethany sounded happy and a touch flirtatious, knocking James further off kilter. "I was looking in my phone for James Connerton—no one you would know—but as I scrolled through the Jameses I saw your name and couldn't resist."

The rest of the conversation, though brief, blurred as James tried to make sense of what was happening.

Even odder was that he *did* know a James Connerton, though he didn't mention that bit.

He hung up and stared at the phone, feeling light-headed. *Probably need to eat. Sandwich would be good—tuna and . . .*

He was interrupted by his new coworker Gary, leaning into his office.

"I'm heading to BJ's. You want a sandwich?"

"BJ's?"

"You know, deli around the corner."

James looked at him suspiciously. "What the hell's going on?" He sounded almost angry.

Gary looked at him sideways. "Lunch? You know, mid-day meal? You okay? You look a little . . . I don't know. Freaked out."

"Yeah, sorry, I didn't mean to sound—never mind. It was just . . ." He sighed, hung his head a moment, then looked up and smiled. "Sandwich would be great. Thanks. I could really go for tuna and turkey on a roll. Tomatoes, lettuce, pickles, hold the mayo and mustard."

Gary stared at him. "No shit. Really?"

"I know, it's an odd combo—"

"Are you kidding?"

"No, I—"

"Best combo ever! I thought I was the only one in the world who eats tuna and turkey." He laughed. "That's amazing. And cool. Better with mustard though. The guy at BJ's thinks I'm nuts. Good to know I'm not the only one who knows a good sandwich combo." He shook his head as he walked out.

James started to wonder if stuff like this used to happen as frequently when he wasn't paying attention. He was still trying to get used to the idea that what seemed like coincidences might instead be sticky notes from the Universe. He was decidedly unclear what the messages could be trying to tell him. He was just as unclear about who or what this Universe with the capital U was supposed to be, and whether Phil was part of a cult, or maybe some new age religion.

Life was getting harder to pin down, reality less reliable. He kept telling himself to go with the flow—very California. In the Midwest, he would've been laughed out of the office using that phrase. Not yet sure how the woo-woo meter would register here in Princeton. He knew from recent reading that some significant consciousness research was happening at the university. Whether people were comfortable talking about it—or even knew about it—was another thing altogether.

He glanced at the clock. It was 1:11—that was another thing. When he checked the time it was frequently 1:11 or 11:11 or 2:22. Numbers lined up everywhere he turned, like they were under orders. It was starting to feel like a cosmic joke. *The kind of thing Cal would get off on. Maybe he's come back to haunt me.*

At 1:23, Gary returned with sandwiches and sat across from

him, unwrapping his own tuna and turkey. "You want to try it with spicy mustard? You're missing out." He held out the half of his sandwich he hadn't touched yet.

"Thanks, but I rarely do condiments." He took a bite and chewed thoughtfully. "Hey Gary, do you notice . . ." *How do I ask this without sounding crazy?* Gary watched him.

"What?"

"I'm just wondering if you notice patterns . . ."

"What kind of patterns? Like in carpets you mean, or wallpaper? I don't get what you're asking." He took another huge bite, mustard lingering on the edge of his upper lip.

"No, like time, for example. Like when you look at the clock it's 11:11 or 2:22 or like when you buy something and the total is $45.67, you know like the numbers are . . . well, they don't appear random, like you'd expect." He stuffed his mouth to keep from saying anything more to further embarrass himself.

"Not really." Gary squinted at him. "Maybe you have some kind of disorder. You know, like numeralitis."

James covered his mouth to keep from spitting out his lunch as he burst into laughter.

Gary smiled. "Actually, it does happen every so often. I kind of like it. Makes me feel like when I was a kid with a secret decoder ring."

"I had one of those. Cracker Jacks, wasn't it?" Gary nodded. "A couple weeks ago, I felt like I was somehow catching the rhythm of my life. *Surfing the life wave.*"

"What do you mean?"

James set down his sandwich and wiped his mouth with a napkin. "It was like—like I'd arrive at the bus stop at precisely the moment the bus did, even if I thought I was ahead of schedule or running late."

"Nice! Wish I could make that happen."

"Yeah. But it wasn't something I could make happen. Like I could surf the wave, but not control the wave. I tried—the results were pretty disastrous."

"What happened?"

"Everything went wrong—alarm didn't go off, I missed my bus—despite being right on time according to the bus schedule."

"Was that last Monday?"

"Yep."

"I remember you coming in pissed. We all steered clear."

"Went downhill from there. Worst day I've had in a long time." He bit into his sandwich, and they chewed in silence.

Gary wiped a glob of mustard from the corner of his mouth. "Some days really suck. I've had plenty like that. Feels like everything goes wrong. But then usually the next day is better."

"It was such a shift from things going so smoothly that it felt like a bait and switch. So that night I went to a movie—a psycho-thriller—but ended up so disturbed by the film I had trouble sleeping."

"I know that routine."

"So, Tuesday I was determined not to repeat that. Didn't set an alarm, dragged through the morning, missed the bus."

"You looked like hell."

"Thanks."

"Just saying."

"Turned out almost as bad as Monday. Except I was so exhausted I fell asleep without even eating dinner."

"Seems like you've been pretty upbeat since though. Well, until you barked about lunch."

"Sorry about that. Funny thing is, the less I think about it, the better off I seem to be—except for noticing when things go well."

"My dad always says, 'You want to have a good day? Make it one. Start with an attitude of gratitude.' He grew up in the Bronx: 'attitude of gratitude,'" Gary repeated, adding his dad's signature hand gesture to the accent.

"My dad was more a coach—you can do it! Rise to the challenge! Slay the dragon! Conquer the world! He had a million of them. But seems like the world doesn't want to be conquered. I guess it would rather we calmed down."

"And be grateful."

"And be grateful. I like that."

"Your dad sounds like he spent some time in the Army—be all that you can be."

"Yeah. He was a good guy. So, don't work at it and notice when things go well."

"And be grateful."

"And be grateful," James repeated.

"Not much to work with." Gary scrunched up his deli paper and bag and tossed it from the doorway into the trash across the room. "Score!" He pounded the door frame in victory, jiggling the white board beside it where James's sales goals shouted for attention in large red numbers.

James lived and died by those goals—had mastered them. But those were the result of taking specific actions, making lists and calls and following up. Those you could map out and have some control over. This idea of intention that he'd been reading about was a different beast. Goals he understood. Intention was a mystery.

No time to go down that rabbit hole now though. He wouldn't hit his current goal without doing the requisite calls. He scanned his list. At James Connerton his mouth twisted sideways into a mystified grin. *If Cal were alive, I'd be convinced this was a huge practical joke being pulled on me. Maybe it is.* He started dialing. *Maybe it is.*

CHAPTER 11

Little Thanks

HANNAH

The sticky note on her mirror was spattered with toothpaste, but its message had wormed its way into Hannah's life. Each morning she tried to think of something to be grateful for with each step from her bed to the bathroom. Warm toes. Job. Maudie. Whole wheat pastry flour. Coconut sugar. Almond milk. Chocolate . . . *Okay, now it's just making me hungry.*

Her shower brought gratitude, too. For hot water. Steamy mirrors. Even the towel's squeak as she cleared a spot with it. But in that clearing her eyes grew wide when she saw, looking back, the eyes of her seventeen-year-old self. Her mind somersaulted back to the time she'd fled into a pounding waterfall of scalding water to escape her parents' fighting. In that mirror Hannah had looked deep into other eyes. Kind eyes. Calmer eyes. At seventeen she didn't know whose. Twenty-nine years later, she realized it had been her future self, as if time had folded in on itself.

How distinct the two Hannahs felt! They studied each other—skin, eyelashes, pupils. Fear stared longingly into peace. Gratitude reached back through the fold to offer comfort. Neither wanted to blink and sever the connection. They wanted to touch but dared not move. The older yearned to send wisdom—but the younger had not cultivated a field to receive it yet. The moment called for no action, just the willingness to be fully present.

Wisdom is s*imply being. Not facts, not advice on teabag tags.* Her
lips formed the words "Bless you." Breath re-fogged the circle
she'd rubbed, but the rest of the mirror had cleared to reflect her
damp, naked body. Toned and fit. And the scar on her left shoulder to remind her of the crash when she was eighteen. Her eyes
flicked back to warn of the accident to come—to reassure her that
she would be okay, that she'd get through it.

A knock on the door startled them both. When she looked
back, the younger Hannah was gone. She rubbed her fingers
across the four-inch scar at the top of her collar bone.

"Hannah? You alright in there?" Maudie's voice, tinged with
concern.

Hannah wrapped herself in the towel and peeked out. "Sorry,
didn't mean to hog the bathroom."

"You weren't, but you been in there a while, so I was jus' makin'
sure you're okay." Maudie looked startled. "My Lord, now that's a
scar with a story if I ever did see one."

"Got time for tea?" Hannah asked.

"Kettle's already on."

"I'll get dressed. Down in a flash."

"Got some of that lapis sue song tea you said you like."

"Lapsang Souchong. Perfect. Thank you!" Hannah padded off
to her room.

A few minutes later, cupping steaming mugs, Hannah on the
loveseat, feet tucked in next to her, puppy slippers napping on
the floor, Maudie seated in the Olive waiting patiently, Hannah
searched for the end of her memory's skein.

"Mom and Dad took me out for my eighteenth birthday," she
began. "Dad had already had a few too many beers. As usual. He
ordered one for me too—as if turning eighteen meant nothing
but permission to drink legally. Woohoo! But I refused to touch
it. So he drank that one, too."

"Sounds like trouble was brewin', so to speak."

"Cute, Maudie, thanks. My tale kneaded that little bit of

leavening," Hannah enacted making bread as Maudie groaned. "When we left, I offered to drive, but he wouldn't let me. 'What, you think just because you're fuckin' eighteen I'm letting you drive?'"

Maudie scowled. "He always talk to you like that?"

"Whenever he was drinking. Which was most of the time. I tried to point out that I hadn't had any alcohol, that I was like a designated driver. And that I thought *maybe*—and he's like 'Fuck what you thought. When I'm in the car, I drive. You got that clear? You should be fuckin' grateful we let you drive at all. You're still a kid, no matter what the law says.' Sorry, Maudie—this scene is seared into my memory in technicolor—including each expletive."

"He's the one should be apologizin', not you."

"I mumbled a response, even though I knew better than to say anything. Mom had long ago thrown away her own life for the safety of silence. But I'd already provoked him. 'A car is not a goddamn toy. Teenagers get killed all the time in cars 'cause they don't know what the fuck they're doing. You should be grateful I'm driving. Especially in this fuckin' rain.'"

"It was rainin'?"

"Pouring. A deluge."

"Mm-mm." Maudie shook her head.

"Mom said his name—her way of letting me know she was on my side, though she wouldn't go to bat for me—not even on my birthday. He yelled and turned, boring his *look* into her. She wilted. Put her water bottle to her mouth to take a drink—almost as if that would help."

"Makes my blood boil when men do that. Shuttin' women down."

"While he's giving Mom the look, I'm in the back seat seeing brake lights coming at us fast. Too late when he saw them. He wrenched the steering wheel. The last thing I remember was the tires screeching and the sound. That sound—it drowned out everything, filled my dreams for months. Invaded my bones."

"Sounds like you're lucky to be alive."

"That's what everyone told me. I woke up in the hospital with stitches in my shoulder and a severe concussion. To a life I didn't recognize."

"Lord have mercy."

"The car was wrapped around a pole. They needed the jaws of life to extricate us. That's what they told me. I was unconscious—thank goodness."

"An' it was your birthday?"

"Yep, April first. Happy birthday to me."

"April? That's comin' up, we can—"

"Thanks, but it's not a day I celebrate. April Fool. My gift that birthday was an entirely new life. Not quite the gift I'd expected, maybe not what I'd asked for."

"But maybe what you needed," Maudie said gently.

"Maybe." Hannah sat quietly, sipping her tea. "Maybe so. Want to hear something really crazy? Mom drowned. That drink of water she took to deflect Dad's glare—the bottle was wedged by the airbag. They said she was probably unconscious so couldn't do anything about it. But her death certificate said she drowned."

"Death takes us all kinds of ways."

"My Grandma said she'd been drowning for years, living with Dad. I remember Mom once telling me he hadn't always been like that—that alcohol made him mean. Which is why I stayed away from it." The tender silence provided space for their thoughts. "For months after, Dad's last words rang in my head like a bad case of tinnitus: 'You should be fuckin' grateful.' The irony is that's what I'm finally trying to do—be grateful."

She set her tea down and leaned forward. "Sometimes it feels like it takes everything I can muster just to take a deep breath. I mean, without tightening up. I just want to cry or kick something. But I can't even do that without my mind declaring how stupid it all is. How stupid I am. And then my father's voice roars in my head—stupid this, stupid that, stupid Hannah." She picked up her mug again and swirled the tea ball before setting it in a small bowl.

"We start out believin' whatever we're told—true or not. Course we do."

"What did your parents tell you?"

"'bout what?"

"About you."

Maudie looked up to her left and smiled. "Mama called me her little miracle—Miracle Maudie. She'd miscarried several times, so it felt like a miracle that she carried me full term. I tried to live up to that name, though didn't always feel I deserved it." Maudie glanced at the clock in the corner. "And speakin' of miracles, it'll be one if I get to the bank before it closes. I'll see you later."

"I'll clear up the tea things."

"Thank you."

"No problem."

"I mean for sharin' your story. For lettin' me in."

Hannah responded haltingly, realizing as she said it how much it meant to her. "Thank you for listening. For caring."

Maudie's smile warmed the room.

The next day Hannah took advantage of the gorgeous weather and went for a ride. Buoyant from yesterday's conversation, she pedaled over to see Jaz, who was hunched over in the garden with a trowel in hand.

"Hi!" Hannah called out, straddling her bike.

"Oh!" She stood and stretched her back out. "You startled me. What are you up to?"

"Nothing. Enjoying the day. What are those?" Hannah nodded toward a potted plant.

"I don't remember. Lost the tag. But they are supposed to grow

THE LEFT TURN

tall and have yellow flowers. I like yellow."

"Me too. Reminds me of forsythia, but I don't know if that grows out here. In New Jersey, when I was little, I used to hide from my dad under the forsythia bush. Spring and summer it was like a little fairy house, bright yellow on stems branching over me. He never found me there."

"I had a tree house. Wasn't really *in* a tree—I was too little to be climbing trees. But we had some big logs that were arranged so there was an enclosed space. You want to sit a minute? My back could use a break." They sat on the steps and watched a trail of ants move in an orderly line across the sidewalk.

"I rode out to the beach a couple days ago and there was this big driftwood log that invited me to sit. Funny to hear myself say it that way—invited me to sit." Jaz smiled slyly but didn't interrupt. "All I could hear were gulls and waves. And there were cracks in the log that—that made me wish I was small enough to crawl inside and disappear. To leave everything behind, to stop thinking, to stop being me. Or to change into something so much simpler—like an ant. Do you ever feel like that?"

"Every day. It's why I meditate. So I can be simpler. To shut out the noise."

"Really? But . . . you always seem so calm, so peaceful. Like you wouldn't need to meditate."

"Yeah, well . . . that's because I do."

"Could you show me?"

"What?"

"How to meditate?"

Jaz squirmed. "Not really . . ."

Hannah looked offended. "Oh . . . okay . . ."

"I mean, it's—it's not something you *do*. It's more like *not* doing than *doing*."

"You just said you meditate. So, you must be doing something. But if it's some kind of secret or something, that's fine . . ."

"No, it's not a secret, it's just . . . I'm just a student myself." Jaz was starting to feel frustrated too. "Okay, we can try. Close your eyes."

"Now? Doesn't it take a long time?"

"What? No. There's no time limit. Even a minute helps."

"Oh. Okay."

"Close your eyes. Now just focus on your breath going in and out."

Hannah took a long slow breath and let it out. She opened her eyes. "Now what?"

"Now nothing. Just—just close your eyes. And breathe. Stop doing everything else and just pay attention to your breath."

Hannah kept her eyes closed but fidgeted, suddenly itchy in one spot on her cheek. Then another on her leg. Her throat felt dry. A mosquito buzzed her ear. "How long do I keep my eyes closed?"

Jaz sighed. "Just take three long slow breaths and focus on the sensations of it coming and going." To her surprise, Hannah visibly relaxed further with each breath. "Okay, you can open your eyes."

"That's meditation?"

"Well, it's a start."

"What's next?"

"Just practice being still. Not just your body, but your mind too. The hard part is to stop thinking."

"How do you stop thinking?"

"You can't, but with practice you can get better at not getting hijacked by every thought that comes down the pike."

"Sounds impossible. I can keep my thoughts to myself, no problem, but getting my mind to actually shut up? That's beyond anything I can imagine. How do you do it?"

"Just focus on the sensations—really focus. Intensely—like your life depends on it. Let thoughts pass through, come and go. Keep bringing your attention back to your breath." Jaz stood. "Speaking of which, I need to get this in the ground so I can get to class on time."

"Okay, I'll leave you to it." As she swung her leg over her bike she asked, "What kind of class?"

Jaz smiled. "Meditation."

"Seriously?"

"Yeah. You can come if you want, but it's an hour of meditation. Then a talk. Think you're ready to jump in the deep end?"

"An hour? Wow. Is it every week?"

"Yeah."

"Any tests to take or papers to write?"

"No, of course not."

"What if I fall asleep?"

"Just no snoring. Or I'd be forced to elbow you."

"Maybe after I'm back from my book tour next month. My publisher has me on a short tour on the East Coast."

"Wow, that's great!"

"Sounds exciting, but makes me so nervous."

"I'm sure your audiences will love you."

"I don't mean that. I mean flying."

"Well, maybe starting to meditate will help make that less stressful. Come next week."

"You sure?"

"Go into training, try a few minutes a day to get yourself warmed up for it. Start with three breaths at a time and add another breath each time."

"You're on."

"Meet me here at 6:30."

"Thanks for letting me come along. I'll try not to embarrass you."

"It'll be nice to go with a friend."

Hannah pedaled off, feeling more loved than she could ever remember. Like a flower was blooming inside her. She committed to keeping it watered.

CHAPTER 12

Reflections

JAMES

James reached automatically for his mug. A light brown swirl of cream clung to the inside, a ring where the surface had cooled at an unusual angle. He must have left it tipped half off the coaster, half on the oak desk it should be protecting. It had gone cold, and he liked his coffee steaming. He studied the cream ring a moment before heading toward the microwave in the office kitchen.

"Jim!"

He stopped and swung around to Dan's doorway.

"You coming out for drinks?" He'd been in the office eight weeks but had only met the director of CRG's Princeton division yesterday, a man in his mid-forties.

"Tonight?"

"Yeah. Ivy Inn." Dan came over to the door. "Sort of a dive. But it has character. Your girlfriend's welcome to join us."

"Girlfriend?"

"Boyfriend, whatever. Didn't you say you had a partner?"

"I don't think so." James looked again at the skewed ring of cooled cream. *Two smoky-blue mugs in a stainless sink.*

"Well, you oughta know."

"No partner."

"Whatever you say." Dan winked as he organized papers on his desk. "How long were you in the Bay Area?"

"A few months. I was ready."

"Breaking up can do that, especially the ones you'd rather forget." Dan dropped a mess of papers in the center of the desk. "I can use some coffee too. Let's go." Dan stopped at another office. "Marilyn, be an angel and organize that mess of paperwork on my desk, would you?"

"I've got my own work, Dan. You didn't hire me to be your secretary." Among four mid-fortyish men, Marilyn, the only woman, held her own, though she was almost young enough to be their daughter.

As they entered the kitchen, James said, "Not sure another cup of coffee is a good idea. But unless you've got a space heater, I'll take it just to keep my fingers functional. I thought the office in San Francisco was cold—don't you guys turn on the heat?"

Gary slipped into the kitchen for a refill as well.

Dan poured them both steaming coffee. "It's on. This charming old manor has an antiquated heating system but can't get an upgrade. It would alter an historic landmark. Historical Society! People clinging to the past are preserving nothing but our freezing butts."

Gary interjected, "Dan, you know that's B.S. You're just a cheap Philistine. James, I always have an extra sweater lying about if you need one." He retired back to his office, cradling the warmth of his mug and shaking his head.

Dan poured cream into his cup. "Wear layers. You'll get used to it."

"I thought by April it would be warm. Spring, you know?"

"Normal went out with climate change. We're not in Kansas anymore."

"Weird."

"Yep."

"No, I mean that reference. It's like it . . . Never mind." James dismissed the coincidence—or whatever it was.

The kitchen window looked out through leafless branches,

hopeful green leaf buds, timid with uncertainty. It was only 4:00, but pedestrians—collars turned up against the chill—were sparse as dark clouds crept in. The weather report had warned of temperatures dropping though the day.

"Don't you worry, Jim—"

"James."

"You don't mind if I call you Jim, right? Don't you worry about caffeine. A few beers and you'll sleep plenty soundly." James sighed.

"Let's finish up and get the hell out of here," Dan said as he walked back into his office. "You want a ride to the Ivy?"

"I've got a car. Text me the address and I'll meet you there."

"Will do. You're gonna love this place, loaded with eye candy— college girls. Hey, no harm in enjoying the view. By the way, how's the search for that start-up CFO coming? Did you reach that Fizzy guy?"

James had been on the phone all day to consultants about job openings—their availability, who they might know with the skill set he was seeking. Building relationships. "Fisby. Not yet, but I've got a few new leads to check out. Connerton is looking like a possibility." As James closed his door and returned to his desk, he heard Dan pleading again for Marilyn's help.

Warming his hands with the fresh French roast—steam rising, swirling and vanishing—he took the time to observe it. *Where did it go?* He couldn't remember the last time he'd slowed down enough to notice the beauty of the phenomenon. It was mystical, magical as a white rabbit disappearing in a top hat with the wave of a wand. He cherished the memories of his mother reading *Alice in Wonderland* to him. He was grateful that she'd passed when she did.

He turned to the window. Daylight was dwindling beneath the cloud cover. His reflection looked back at him, pondering their relationship, and he drank in symmetry with himself. Haroche and Wineland had won a Nobel Prize for proving that something could be in two places at the same time. Maybe he was doing that—or *being* that. What if I could close the gap between how I feel—this burning inside, and the guy in the reflection who looks so serene? Is the reflection really me too? *If life is really our perception of it, maybe I'm the reflection and that guy is me.*

It suddenly occurred to him that he hadn't actually seen his own face since he was a teenager. His thick beard had eclipsed it all his adult life. An urge to see himself rose fiercely, quickly forming itself into a decision. He smiled broadly.

To the right of the window, next to the colonial wall sconce was a photo of mountains reflected in a still lake. He'd picked it up at a local gallery after his first day facing the blank paneled wall. When he'd hung it, he had to check the wire across the back to determine which way was up. *Had the framer only guessed? What had the photographer seen? Do we see in three dimensions, or is that the brain's post-production interpretation?*

The book on the birth of quantum physics had nudged awake his inner child—dangling from the mental monkey bars of possibility. Diving into rabbit holes of reality, particles vanishing to reappear in another time and place—far more exciting than half dollars appearing behind his ear. *We have this experience of living yet know so little about what it really is.*

James tilted his head to view the photo sideways, imagining a mirrored world on its side. He suddenly vaulted out of his seat as hot coffee splashed onto his thigh. *Stupid!* A flash of Cal laughing at him, flaring an impulse to throw the mug across the room. *Matching blue mugs. Fragments scattered on a tiled floor. A woman with golden hair mopping it up, sobbing. Who was that woman?*

The phone rang. Private number.

Maybe a call on that CFO position. He took a breath and engaged his business demeanor. "CRG, this is James. May I help you?"

"James Wescott?" A young woman. She sounded uneasy.

His shoulders tensed in reply. "Yes."

"Who used to live in Union, New Jersey?"

Wary, he replied cautiously, "Yes . . ."

"This is your daughter, Allie—Allison."

His face suddenly pale, James sank slowly onto his chair, stumbling as it tried to roll out from under him. His breath caught and his mind raced chaotically, searching for a set of words he could assemble into a thought, a response.

But she pressed on. "Don't talk. Don't say anything. Just listen. All I ask is that you don't hang up, because it took everything I've got to make this call and I will hate you for the rest of my life if you hang up."

James's throat was so constricted that he wasn't able to speak anyway.

"Look, Mom told me you tried to talk her into having an abortion, so I get that you didn't want me. And that you bailed on us when I was two. Mom made it extremely clear that you are the world's most uncaring, selfish jerk. But I wanted you to know I am getting married. You don't have to come, and we aren't inviting you anyway. Mom would flip out if we did. But . . . for some reason even I don't understand, I wanted you to know. You're the only dad I have, even though you don't care about me or want me in your life. That's all I wanted to say. So . . . good-bye."

"Wait!" But the call had ended. James started pressing keys to find the number to call back, but there was no way to call back a private number.

Dan appeared in the doorway, coat on. "Enough for today. Let's get out of here. You ready?"

James blinked.

"Jim?"

He put his phone in his pocket. "Yeah." He grabbed his jacket from the hook.

Dan took his elbow to steer him. "I think you need a drink more than I do. Let's go. It's raining—you got an umbrella or hat or something?"

"No. I've got nothing." *Allison thinks* I *left* them. *Married—my baby's getting married.* A wave of loss crashed over him—a rip tide carrying his heart out to sea.

Dan was pulling out an umbrella to cover them both as he locked the door behind them.

CHAPTER 13

~~Coincid~~—No, "Synchronicities"

HANNAH

The man in the next seat smiled. "Are you alright?" The plane had started to taxi. Hannah was gripping the armrests tightly, trying to remember how to breathe like they taught in meditation class.

"Uh, sure." Hannah snugged her seatbelt tighter.

"You look a little nervous."

"Haven't flown in a while."

"Safer than driving."

"True. Especially since I don't drive." She turned toward the window. A flock of birds crossed the airfield in tight formation—as one, shifting direction up and out of sight. Hannah scanned the skies for them, needing a distraction from the roil in her belly.

She could feel him watching her. "How do you get around?" She turned, annoyed but not wanting to be rude. "If I may ask . . . especially in the Bay Area?"

"Bike, bus, walk. Not so hard—just takes more time."

"I'm impressed. And please forgive my footnote: flying is also safer than biking."

"What are you—some kind of airline safety advocate or something?"

"No, I'm not on the public side of things, more behind the scenes. Statistics analyst. Transportation happens to be my current specialty."

Hannah settled back. "Seriously? 'Current specialty' . . . does that mean you had another one?"

"I'm reinventing myself all the time. I think we all are to a degree. Why limit ourselves when we have so much potential."

"I guess."

"You don't sound convinced."

"Every time I've been told I have 'so much potential,' it's been a back-handed way of saying I'm failing at life. 'You have so much potential.' The unspoken appurtenant statement is: 'It's a shame to see you wasting it.'"

Feeling awkward and vulnerable after her blurtation, Hannah tried to extricate herself. "Excuse me," she called to a passing flight attendant checking seat backs and belts, "when you get a chance might I have a pillow?" He pulled one from the overhead bin as they started to taxi. The man beside her had to sit back to accommodate the exchange, but he wasn't ready to let go of the conversation.

"Who told you that?"

Hannah looked out the window before turning back to answer. "High school guidance counselor. Decades ago, but unforgettable." She tried to plump the absurdly small pillow, but it just made her feel more ridiculous.

"Guess that counselor gave you something to rise above." She stopped pummeling. She hadn't ever thought about it that way.

He smiled and pulled out a book, tilting the cover toward her. "Have you read this?"

"Oddly enough, I just finished it. Great twist at the end."

"No spoilers please."

"I would never."

"I love that it takes place in Princeton, where I grew up. PJ's Pancakes, where the detective hangs out, was my favorite haunt. Ever been?" She shook her head, relieved with the change of subject. "I'm Brad, by the way."

"Weird."

"What's weird about my name?"

"Nothing at all. It was my father's. I haven't met any other Brads. But mostly weird because Princeton is where I'm headed." She tucked the pair of coincidences into a pocket in her mind for later consideration.

"Guest lecturer at the University?"

"I'm on tour to peddle my book. My first book," she added for accuracy. And modesty. "My only book."

"You're an author?" Hannah smiled and nodded, starting to relax. He looked expectant. "And you go by . . . ?"

"Hannah."

He waited for the last name, but she appeared to be done. "Are you a single-name author? Or a rare humble one?" Her face twisted into a question mark. "Authors generally tell you their pen name, their website, and the plot to every novel they've ever written to elicit a promise you'll buy one as soon as possible—or else they have a few copies in their carryon just in case. You might just be the first humble author I've met."

"Could be all the ones that aren't so bold are hidden away writing in self-imposed solitary confinement."

"Hm. Hadn't considered that."

"I'm Hannah Fleet. Cookbook. No novels—yet—I don't think. Maybe someday. Mystery probably."

"You're kidding, right?"

"Why would I be kidding?"

"Is that your real name?"

"Why would I lie?"

"Hannah Fleet's Better Eats?"

"Wait—you've heard of it?"

"I just ordered it for my daughter!"

"Oh my God. What a coincid— synchronicity!" She stopped herself, pictured Jaz smiling. She tucked this one in the pocket with the others.

"Amazing. It got great reviews! I'm honored to meet the real

Hannah Fleet." After a moment he added, "And clearly you did it."

"Did what?"

"You rose above that stupid guidance counselor's comment. Best-selling author—well done!"

"Thanks." The engines roared to lift off. Hannah cringed.

"Flying makes you nervous?" She nodded. "Well, you're not alone. About forty percent of the general population feels that way, statistically speaking."

"I didn't know there were so many of us. My publisher made all the arrangements, or I'd be home baking mango sour cream scones. I'm actually hoping this trip will prepare me for next summer. I'm going to London—to visit my daughter." Saying those words made it feel more real to her, and chatting was calming her nerves. After a while they settled into a comfortable silence. For most of the flight she was able to sleep, partly thanks to exhaustion from her fitful night of packing and pre-flight anxiety, and partly due to the kindness of this stranger.

At the busy security checkpoint at Newark airport, a liveried driver—bouncing with surprising eagerness—was holding high a sign with her name. They collected her baggage—all present and accounted for. "Good flight, Ms. Fleet?" the driver asked as they pulled into traffic.

"It was, thanks. I get uncomfortable around strangers sometimes, and I worry about baggage and stuff, so travelling can be a bit nerve-wracking."

"You can sit back and relax. Everything's my responsibility now!"

She inhaled deeply. "Something smells really good."

The driver blushed. "I baked Chocolate Almond Crisps—from your book. I was thinking you might like some after your trip, but then chickened out on offering them to you. They're here if you want, but please don't feel like you need to accept them. It was a dumb idea."

"That's so kind of you, thank you. I'd actually love to try one. Airplane food is—well, just that."

He handed her the box of cookies. The familiar taste comforted her. "Delicious. You enjoy baking?"

"I considered it as a career. Attended culinary school for a year. But being in a commercial kitchen terrified me. Was always afraid I'd burn the place down or poison someone."

"Can I assume that didn't happen?"

"It didn't, but I'm driving a cab not baking. Driving's okay—and I'm grateful to have an income—but it's not what I'd say is my calling or my greatest gift or passion. Don't worry, though, I'm a really good driver." His eyes smiled at her in the rearview mirror.

"I'm just kind of blown away that you're a chef."

"I'm a big fan of your book. I've probably done ninety percent of the recipes."

"You're kidding—no one does that."

"I do. I think it's an OCD thing. That's what my partner says, but then he loves eating what I bake, so he's a happy camper."

They rode in silence for a while, Hannah kneading the synchronicities in her mind, pushing them away and then pulling and folding them into her experience, feeling herself stretch and grow and rise.

Slowing at a stoplight, the driver pointed to a billboard shouting in rainbow colors "Awaken to Oneness."

"See there? If we really are all one, then I guess we don't have to worry about strangers." He laughed.

Hannah smiled. Oneness was one of Jaz's favorite topics, but Hannah regularly stubbed her toe on the concept. "I can accept the idea that we're all energy, but beyond that . . ."

"Yeah. The idea of being related to some people I meet is enough to give me the heebie-jeebies. Being the same as them . . . How could we be?" They drove past a collection of tents on an embankment. A shirtless guy waved as they passed. She lifted her hand to wave back. *Could they be?* Hannah hovered at the edge of the rabbit hole, cautiously peering in, drawn by her yearning for a better world.

At the hotel, the driver unloaded Hannah's bags and handed her a card. "If you need a ride anywhere, here's my number. Your publisher has us scheduled for all the official rides, but if you need anything else local, it's on me. You have a good night, Ms. Fleet."

"Hannah, please."

"You have a good night, Hannah."

She glanced at his card. "Thanks, Theo. You too." He drove off, leaving Hannah in a warm glow of gratitude.

Warned of freezing rain, Hannah wore a fuzz-lined raincoat and was grateful for the wave of warm air that crashed over her as she slipped in the door at Cooke's Book Nook. The darkness of the afternoon made the well-lit interior welcoming.

Twenty-five sturdy oak chairs were set up to the left of the front door, most filled or reserved with a coat hanging over the back. A poster-sized cover of her cookbook was displayed on a metal stand centered on a table that was covered with a festive cloth. Beside it sat an enlargement of the Coconut Dreams recipe, behind a platter of cheese, grapes, and the highlighted cookies. Off to the side, glasses and wine encouraged the audience to stick around after the talk.

Hannah pulled up the sagging ankle socks of her childhood fears and looked around the room full of strangers. *Every friend is first a stranger.* She reassured herself by thinking of Maudie and Jaz, then, from her day of travel, of Brad, her seat mate, and Theo, her driver.

A young woman approached. Her name tag told Hannah this was Jenny, the manager with whom she'd spoken last week.

"Hannah, welcome. How was your trip? Everything went smoothly, I hope?"

"Yes, thanks."

Jenny took her coat. "I'll put it on the coat rack for you. Looks dry. No rain yet?"

"Not yet, but it feels imminent."

"Well, it doesn't seem to have kept your fans away. Come on in." Jenny led the way toward the front table. A small group of young women chatted on without noticing. An elderly couple browsing near the back saw her and worked their way to their seats. People who were already seated adjusted position. Lining up like iron filings responding to a magnetic pull, the patrons organized themselves, their breathing patterns synchronizing, eyes and minds refocusing, shoulders and knees pointing toward Hannah at the front of the room.

She'd never noticed such coordination before, but there was something happening that felt charged.

As the group aligned their focus, she suddenly *felt* how they were all one—one unified diversely-expressed being. *It's like the orderly marching of ants. Like a flock of birds in formation. It's our attention that brings us together, revealing our oneness.*

Jenny joined Hannah, beaming. "Welcome everyone and thanks for coming out, despite the impending storm. Must be the smell of cookies drifting out the door. *There's* a lesson in marketing for me! Today we are excited to have Hannah Fleet, author of *Hannah Fleet's Better Eats,* joining us all the way from San Francisco." Jenny did her promotional pitch for the store and their author series, then rattled off a short bio of Hannah that the publisher had emailed. Hannah did not recognize herself in the words that drifted and scattered, dropping into the laps of the eager audience.

Allie was mentioned and her name tickled the group of young women. The history being strewn about the room was one Hannah had never heard before. If she had lived any of it, it was so far removed that she could not in good conscience own it. But she had nothing to replace it with. The funny thing was that all her anguish over her disconnected past was starting to feel irrelevant. At least less relevant than who she was now.

Welcoming applause snapped her back to Cooke's Book Nook. A wave of gratitude for all these people sharing this moment, this space, and a love for fixing good food swept over her.

"My mom used to say to me every night at dinner, 'You better eat, Hannah Fleet.' I never dared talk back to her, but every night I'd think, 'I'd eat if it tasted better.'" She paused at their unexpected laughter. "Now I'm grateful to my mother for being such a lousy cook because it drove me, out of desperation, to learn how to prepare yummy food.

"The kitchen has always been my safe space, a place where I could bake up a double batch of comfort, the place where I knew how things worked. In college, I shared a house with several girlfriends. We blasted music and sang and danced around the kitchen, whipping up delicious food we ate together around a beat-up oak table with burn rings."

Hannah was in the zone. She was in the kitchen, measuring response, whipping up interest, stirring stories, simmering engagement, and pulling out of the oven a delicious success. The applause at the end was emphatic. Hannah smiled and bowed her head slightly. The alignment had produced something the audience was attributing to her. Gratitude coursed through her.

The plastic wrap had been removed from the refreshments, but the line to buy the book and have it signed was busiest. A young woman with straight auburn hair stepped forward, one of the chatty ones Hannah had noticed when she first entered. "Ms. Fleet, I don't know if you remember me, but I went to school with Allie in Philadelphia the year before she left on tour. I used to come over and bake with you and her. Those were some of my favorite times because my mom hardly even let me in the kitchen, except to set the table or wash dishes."

Hannah wanted to remember. "What's your name?"

"Molly Ingram. I don't expect you to remember, really. But it meant a lot to me, so I want to thank you. The way you put in each recipe how it makes you *feel*, not just taste—I mean, I get it. I totally get it. Like, our feelings connect us, and food brings us together and it's just—wow! So, when I saw you were coming, I told my friends." She turned and pulled two girls behind her forward with their books. "I convinced them to ditch work and come with me." The other girls set their books next to Molly's for signing. "This is Chris and Annabelle."

"I hope you don't lose your jobs because of me," Hannah tried to look appalled.

"No worries. Mid-afternoon is slow anyway. But dinner rush will be starting soon, so we have to run. But thank you SO much."

"Where do you work?"

"I work at The Princeton Inn. One of those fancy restaurants. Tips are great."

"That's where I'm staying!"

"Awesome! I'll look out for you." Hannah handed Molly's copy to her. "I'll Facebook Allie that I was here. She'll freak. Thanks!" The trio waved and dashed out.

By the time the line had dissipated, the refreshments had been mostly devoured and it was getting dark outside. Jenny was chatting happily with some attendees. Hannah's mind drifted back to what Molly had said. *Feelings. . . Attention . . . Connection . . .* A loud crack of thunder broke into Hannah's thoughts. Jenny was waving to her as a couple dashed out with coats pulled up over their heads.

"Hannah, that was great! Thank you so much. That's the best turnout we've ever had for a cookbook event."

"Thank you! You know, I've always wanted to try my hand at fiction, a mystery with a protagonist who is a chef or a baker. There are some rather gruesome opportunities."

Jenny smiled. "Sounds very Sweeney Todd."

"True. Though recently I've been less inclined towards the darker side of life."

"Well, that's probably a good sign. From what I've read, you had a rough jolt into adulthood, losing your parents on your eighteenth birthday."

"Not as hard as the years leading up to that day! At least in terms of my father."

"You've certainly come out on top, in spite of him."

"Thanks." She felt some awkwardness, but the compliment warmed her. "I'm not sure where my coat . . ."

"When I heard the first thunder, I had one of the girls call you a cab. Should be here any minute."

"I can walk. I'm close by."

A young woman arrived with Hannah's raincoat. Jenny handed it to her. "Not if you don't have a warmer coat than this, plus umbrella and boots. Looks like the cab's already here. Thank you again, Hannah. You take care!" Jenny waved and turned back to some customers who'd decided to remain in the warmth of the store.

Hannah thanked her and dashed out the door. The bell jingled as she left. A man stood outside huddled under the awning. He watched as Hannah climbed into the taxi and settled her bag next to her. The cab pulled away, dragging the man's gaze behind it. A customer exiting the store held the door for him. Warmth and light from the bookstore beckoned.

CHAPTER 14

Sawubona

JAMES

James checked his watch. 5:30. The date he knew without looking—it was burned into him like a brand. As he walked down Nassau Street with a storm in his gut and the November cold jabbing at him, an incoming tide of grief washed over him. He peered at window displays, desperate for distraction, his mind churning as uncontrollably as the vortex of dead leaves gusting violently around him.

Cal up a tree, dropping on Jimmy, scaring him so he swung hard, angry, ready to fight. But Cal lay face down on the grass, not moving, his mop of sandy hair splayed out like a dishrag.

"Get up, you jerk!" Jimmy poked Cal's sneaker with his boot. Nothing. Every emotional gear ground as he shifted from high into reverse into panic.

A movement on the ground. "Why'd ya hit me?" Cal slowly rolled over and pushed himself up, blood smeared under his nose and on his cheeks. "That hurt. I'm telling when Dad gets home." He ran off unsteadily toward the house.

I thought he was dead. I thought I'd killed him. I thought he was dead . . . He IS dead. . . . Cal is dead.

When the first drops hit him, James flinched and looked up. A car started up in a nearby parking space, turning the rain silver in the headlights. The drops on his clean-shaven face were cold and slushy—on the edge of two potential states: water and ice. A shiver ran through him. After work he'd stopped at the barber with a bold directive. He barely recognized himself when it was over. His face prickled with cold.

To his left, an old-fashioned shop doorbell tinkled. A woman dashed out into a waiting taxi. James stared at her golden hair—illuminated by light from the store as the taxi pulled away. Another customer held the door. James went in, ready for any comfort he could find.

Five or six people were lingering around a table with remnants of snacks. He couldn't read what the signs on the table said, but it looked like there had been quite a spread. Just as well he missed it—his belt had been getting tighter. Maybe time to pay for gym membership, since it was too icy to cycle, but he probably wouldn't use it. Maybe he'd change. On the sales counter was a poster: "Change is the only constant." *Not funny.* Phil would smile and say, "Your thoughts create your world." *Ha ha.*

A woman with a sweet face approached. "Looks like you missed it. Sorry." Her ivory skin reminded him of a Zorn painting he had seen once at the Palace of the Legion of Honor.

"What did I miss?"

"Our Meet the Author event. It's every second Friday. Today we had one of Cooke's Book Nook's cookbooks." *Someone who enjoyed words. Good match for a bookstore.*

"That's a mouthful," he commented.

She smiled. "Touché."

"Well, I don't cook, so I guess it wasn't a great loss. Unless the food was particularly good."

"The Coconut Dreams were amazing, but I'm afraid they've been gobbled up."

"Starting to slush out there."

"Well, we've got plenty of cozy spots for reading—and there are still some snacks. Help yourself." She turned to talk with some other folks near the food.

James watched her chat with an elderly couple, then wandered the perimeter of the seating area.

He found a dark brown easy chair and sat next to a floor lamp with cream-colored pompoms dangling around the bottom—something out of a grandmother's attic. James flicked a couple, watched them swing and resettle as if nothing had ruffled them. He wished he could so easily find equilibrium.

He laid his jacket over the arm and sat a few minutes in the luxury of stillness, letting his eyes close. Letting out a long breath, he opened them to a shelf with titles by Lynne McTaggart, the same author Phil kept raving about. He stood up, chose *The Bond, and* opened it randomly. An italicized word jumped out at him: *Avatar*.

The author was referring to the film and the *Sawubona*—or *we* see you—greeting, pointing out that not only does it reflect the notion that each of us is connected to all living things and all consciousness, but that our connection extends to the past as well. Relating is never a solitary act.

A voice startled him. "How are we doing?"

He looked up at Jenny. Although her use of the word "we" was not so unusual, he couldn't help but hear it in a new way. He hesitated. "We're doing fine. Thanks. Have you read this?" He kept his finger in the book to hold his place as he tilted the cover.

"Not yet. But it's on my list. I have a *long* list. Occupational hazard. I have read one of her other books." She turned toward the shelf and pulled out *The Intention Experiment*. "This one. Fascinating! I was so surprised when she started talking about the research that's being done right here in Princeton. And the global-scale intention experiments she's been leading. So cool." She replaced the book when he didn't reach for it. "What about you?"

Global intention experiments? "Sorry, what do you mean?"

"Have you read any of her books? She did a book signing here a couple years back. Lovely woman."

"Not yet. I bought a copy of this one before I moved from

California, but I must have left it on the plane or something. I think I read the beginning, but never got this far." He flipped it open with his finger. "She mentions *Avatar*—the film—"

"Loved it, saw it in 3D. You must've seen it. It was so popular."

"—but I don't remember this—"

The counter bell chimed. "Oh, sorry, excuse me." She hurried off.

The storm had let up. James checked his watch. It felt like the book was calling to him—again. *Must be time to read it.* Hardly recognizing the thought as his, he carried the book to the sales counter.

CHAPTER 15

Lost Baggage

HANNAH

The two-week book tour had alleviated some of Hannah's travel fears, but booking a flight to London on her own was still nerve-racking. Clicking on the wrong button, missing out on the best price, or belatedly discovering hidden fees put her on edge. With each triple-checked travel detail, she re-checked the price to make sure it hadn't gone up.

Hannah fretted every detail. *If I get on the wrong plane, I could be lost forever.* Even recognizing that fear as irrational, her anxiety about losing her baggage was well-founded, even for non-neurotic travelers. *Is non-neurotic actually a word? I need a* really *cheap plane ticket to London. Stay focused.* An asterisk caught her attention. She scrolled down. *Damn, they charge extra for everything—better bring my own toilet paper and barf bag.*

Annoyed and stressed, Hannah turned away from her new laptop and went downstairs. Maudie had made peanut butter chip brownies that morning before running errands. Hannah pulled in the incipient bulge above her waistband and took two. *I bike enough San Francisco hills that I ought to be able to eat whatever I want.* She put the brownies on a ceramic plate that had a pair of dog paws in the center. Paws. Pause. She did.

She bit into the chewy sweetness. Almond milk would complement them perfectly. Thinking about baggage, she poured a glass, chewed slowly, savored the perfect blend of flavors.

Gradually forming a mental image of the clothes she might need, Hannah slowly climbed the stairs and pictured her suitcases filling up. She liked to pack light for bike trips. *Going to a foreign country means I'll need more stuff, since I'll be further from home. Wait, does that make sense? Maybe I should check a bag and bring extra stuff to avoid getting lost with a bag of dirty underwear in search of a laundromat. But that means baggage fees . . .*

Not that Hannah had to make the baggage decision immediately. But she'd read the fine print, since knowing all the details in advance gave her some small solace. She'd already made a thorough study of the transit systems she'd need upon arrival, and calculated schedules that allowed her time to find her way to Allie's. At least English was the native tongue there. *Thank God. It would have been out of the question if Allie had been touring in Africa or Asia or the like. Or if the visit were to little Lee in China.* Well, that visit would be impossible for reasons Hannah didn't allow her mind to drift into.

Allie had not offered to meet her at the airport, and Hannah hadn't asked her to. Her daughter was independent from an early age—that much was pretty clear—and Hannah would not act like a child to her daughter. Jaz had tried to explain something to her about "acting as if"—as if everything was exactly the way she wanted it. As if her life was just right and all her dreams had come true. Maybe if Hannah acted as if she were okay, at least Allie wouldn't rush her to a therapist before they got through their first cup of Earl Gray—*served with warm scones, jam, and clotted cream.* Hannah pinched some brownie crumbs and kissed them off her fingertips. *Or maybe . . . maybe everything* will *be okay.* Hannah's mind stopped in its tracks. Wherever *that* novel thought came from, it made Hannah smile. It felt good. It felt good to feel good. And to notice that she felt good. An image formed of mirrors facing each other and the endless layers of reflections they created—smiles and good vibes all the way to infinity.

The computer screen went black, her own image staring back at her. She recalled a recent dream, looking at her reflection in a dark window—her face covered with words, questions. A notice popped up that her session had timed out. *Bummer. Uh-oh. Maybe it's a sign that it's a mistake to go. But it seemed like there were signs I should. Maybe it's a sign I need to make a decision!*

An intruder stealing into the shadows of her mind, doubt slipped in through the door left ajar by loitering low self-esteem. *But what if I'm misinterpreting the signs? Or what if they're not signs at all—except of declining mental health. All this business of synchronicities, the idea that they mean something, that they're like clues to the mystery of life—it seemed so cool and exciting at first—like the first day of kindergarten. Go through that door for the first time, and it's a whole new world.*

But once you're through, you find out that what looked like a giant Discovery channel come to life is really a field loaded with landmines of failure. According to the authorities there is only one right answer to each question, which means there are an infinitude of wrong answers. Kaboom! Hannah had grown up doing her best to avoid triggering the landmines set by teachers at school—*kaboom!*—and by parents as she slogged through the homework trenches—*kaboom!* She deployed her arsenal of survival tools: evasion, distraction, and feigned ignorance. As an adult, making decisions and trusting her intuition, which required a foundation of self-confidence, were not her strong suit.

Growing up, Hannah had lost every time at Clue. She was too afraid to guess who killed the victim with what and in which room, because everywhere else in her life it was painful to be wrong. At school she felt like a disappointment. At home she was stupid. With friends it was better to lose—which made them happy—even if it always left her with a stomachache.

If the email about great deals on flights to London at the very moment I first started thinking about it—and not before—was, in fact, a sign, was it necessarily a sign I should go? Does it mean Colonel

Mustard killed Mr. Green in the library with the candlestick or is it just circumstantial evidence and really Colonel Mustard is innocent? What if all this synchronicity stuff is wrong or made up by the same people who created malicious viruses to destroy the computers of people they'd never met? What if we really are just completely separate individuals in a dog-eat-dog world like Konrad Lorenz claimed? What if they're just coincidences that don't mean anything after all? Depression crept closer, settling like dusk.

"Stop!" Hannah shouted. Squeezing her eyes shut, she reminded herself through clenched teeth, "These thoughts do not serve me." Mom shushed her protectively, cooing that *it's just the way it is.* Shaking her head to get the mom in there to lose her footing, she groped in the darkness for something she was grateful for. Her mind went blank. Slowly, a blank chalkboard emerged . . . a piece of chalk in her hand . . . ready to write a list of what she was thankful for. She started to relax into the blankness, imagining she was meditating.

Hannah had only attended a handful of meditation classes with Jaz, not enough to do any good when she was already stressed. But this was what Jaz had told her to do anytime she started to sense panic or depression. She slowed her breath and focused on it. The sun crept over the horizon behind her closed eyes. *Allie.* She smiled. *Allie invited me to visit.* She wrote Allie's name on the blackboard in her mind. *Everything might turn out to be wonderful. We might have a great time together, tramping all over London, catching up, rekindling our relationship.*

The prospect was exciting. She didn't know how long it had been since she'd seen her, but it could've been since their parting when Allie was eight for all Hannah knew. She had vague memories of moving frequently, but none of those blurry images included a child or toys. Kitchens were what mostly came to mind. Lining shelves and drawers with daisies in one sunny kitchen and a beige wheat pattern in one with dark wooden cabinets. And baking. Her mind searched in vain for memories of offering spatulas and mixing bowls with remnants of sweet dough to a young baking assistant to lick clean. *Could everything have happened before she turned eight? Had our entire relationship been squeezed into those few short years?*

One of the recipes in Hannah's cookbook mentioned Allie in the description. "Inspired by my daughter Allie who declared at age four that coconut sugar was her 'favoritest kind of yummer.' At our house sweeteners were known as yummers." This and the encounter with Molly Ingram at the book event in Princeton were Hannah's only clues that their relationship went beyond her limited memories. There lay hope. She added Molly to the blackboard in her mind, then opened her eyes.

Back to the search for flights. She wanted to travel in the summer. *I need time to prepare and save up. I can buy on credit, but I have to be able to pay it off. And I've got that big publishing event in San Francisco next June—maybe I'll land a real job.* Allie had some extra time off around Fourth of July, since it was a U.S.-based touring company, even if the country they were in didn't celebrate the holiday.

Months ago, when the idea of visiting Allie had first come to her, Hannah saw no way to afford it. Over time, the decision to go had solidified. *A leap of faith.* Both Maudie and Jaz had cheered her on when she first voiced the notion. Shortly after that, her publisher had called about a November book tour in New Jersey. Jokingly, Hannah asked if there was a chance of taking the tour to London. Michelle had quipped, "Dream on!" Jaz said that sounded like a clear directive—one Hannah should definitely follow.

She'd had a dream just last night: Allie off in the distance slowly walking away, Hannah running to catch up. But no matter how fast she ran, Allie outpaced her, fog threatening to swallow the blurred figure in the distance. Hannah woke in anguish and certainty—wanting to reconnect with her daughter before it was too late.

Then this morning, she accidentally opened an email she was trying to mark as spam, based on its subject line. Glaring at her was an image that was so like the image from her dream that it unnerved her. The text shouted: "PACK YOUR BAGS! BOOK YOUR TRIP TO LONDON!" It was eerie. A list of hot-linked destinations suggested that she could use airmiles from her book tour. Hannah clicked "London."

A selection of flights populated the screen. Hannah's pocket calendar was open in front of her, having refused to move it to her phone or computer calendar for two reasons: she liked the feel of paper and pencil—she was a writer, after all; and it made her life feel less pixelated, less digital, more—*real.*

She'd written the Publishing Expo West event in ink—a decision based on faith. Staring down her habits, she found ink was the best way to keep her from backing out for all the illegitimate reasons she was so capable of birthing. *Cross-outs are for manuscripts, not for calendars.*

She calculated time for airport security—one hour. Door-to-door shuttle—thirty minutes. Plus extra time in case they are late or traffic is heavy—double it to an hour. Time to get her act together in the morning—one hour. Add some extra for snooze alarm activity in case she had trouble sleeping the night before, which seemed likely—thirty minutes. She added another half hour buffer for good measure and would set her alarm for four hours in advance of flight time. Scrolling to departures after 11:00 a.m., she selected a 12:55 flight out of SFO. She reminded herself with each click of "Continue" that until she entered payment information, she was safe from screwing up anything that would have serious consequences.

Since going overseas for just a week seemed silly, but for as long as two would be expensive, Hannah thought a ten-to-twelve-day trip would be ideal. In the sidebar, she noticed a box to redeem air miles: 50,000 miles for a free international flight. Her balance was nowhere near that.

Damn it! Damn misleading email! They always do that—lead you on like a bait-and-switch, get you all—she stopped, seeing images of Jaz and Maudie telling her that everything works out just the way that's best, even when it looks all wrong.

Hannah closed her eyes and took a deep breath. She added Jaz and Maudie to the gratitude list, then looked at Allie's name at the top. She *wanted* to see Allie, so back to looking for flights. *One step at a time.* She chose dollars, not airmiles. After a thirty-minute struggle holding her anxiety in check about the cost, she heard the door open downstairs. Maudie. Relief. She'd trust Maudie's opinion.

"Maudie!"

"No need to shout—I'm right here." Maudie stood in the doorway, suitcase in hand, smiling broadly.

"You going somewhere?"

"No, silly—you are. Found this for you at Salvation Army."

"You angel! How did you know I was looking at flights?"

"Are you? I didn't. But that's good. Did you book something?"

"I haven't hit the purchase button yet. I haven't even looked at the total yet. Take a look. Then hold my hand while I step off the cliff. Quick—I don't want to time out and have to start over again."

Maudie scrolled down. "I don't get it."

"What?" Hannah panicked. She looked at the screen. The total purchase was $0.00. All the flight info looked right, but it didn't make any sense at all. "Oh, my God. I don't get it either. What did I do wrong?" Her hands went toward the keyboard, but Maudie stopped her.

"Maybe you did something right. Hit the purchase button."

"What? But that can't be right. There must be some mistake."

"I stand as your witness. Hit purchase or I'll do it for you. Hurry up before it changes its mind." Hannah grabbed Maudie's hand for comfort and clicked. The screen congratulated her and promised an email confirmation.

"Shoot!" Maudie hissed.

"What?! You told me to hit purchase!"

"I should've had you add an extra ticket."

"Wait," said Hannah, "let's find out if that was real or an evil trick to empty my bank account." The email confirmed zero. "I still don't get it."

"Maybe it was some computer glitch. But I think I'm going to check flights to New Zealand. I've been wanting to go there ever since I saw the Hobbit movies. Maybe I'll have to find me a suitcase, too!" Maudie dashed into her bedroom. Hannah sat and stared at the email, hardly believing what just happened. Even if she had to pay to check a bag, it wouldn't matter. She emailed Allie the travel itinerary.

The two friends had dinner together, both excited, though Maudie had found no free flights to her dream destination. "You set the intention before Christmas—wasn't it? Just took some months to hatch, looks like. You, Hannah Fleet, are one amazing manifester. I think you owe me some lessons. Free flight to England. Lord have mercy!"

"It didn't feel like I did anything to make it happen. I even started to get indignant that they practically lied about a free flight in their email come-on. But then I imagined what you and Jaz would have said."

"What was that?"

"Everything is just the way it's supposed to be."

"And so it is."

"So I just took a deep breath and kept looking—I really want to go see Allie and maybe free was not how I was going to get to do that."

"Or then again, maybe it was." They laughed over steamed carrots and broiled fish.

Hannah's phone signaled an incoming email. From United Air. She frowned and swallowed her mouthful of carrots. "Uh oh. I was expecting something like this."

137

"Well," Maudie replied, "if you were expecting it, it was likely to come. What is it?"

"Email from United. Probably telling me the *real* cost of the flight I just booked." She read aloud. "It has come to our attention that a flight you booked January 11 at 1:11 Pacific Standard Time was confirmed at a purchase price of $0.00. We discovered a glitch in the online ticketing system that caused several hundred tickets to book at no cost."

Hannah looked up and sighed, dropping her shoulders in dismay. "See? I knew it."

"Keep readin'!"

"As a commitment to our customers and the integrity of our company, United will honor these tickets. Thank you for choosing United. Oh my God!" Hannah's words had slowed as the impact of the message sank in. She had been delivered an amazing gift. *I wonder when the other hundreds of people who got this message set their intentions. What might they have done to pave the way to their dreams? What would Allie say? I wonder what she believes about the Universe and how things work? She started living her dream when she was eight. Maybe she already figured it out.*

Maudie watched as Hannah's face lit up. Like a child discovering that Santa Claus is real after all, that magic and miracles happen every day, and that she can tap into creative power she'd never imagined.

"Wow!" Hannah breathed.

"Wow indeed!"

A fear was already wriggling its way back into Hannah's mind. "What if I lose my baggage?"

Maudie leaned back and squinted at Hannah, crossing her arms. "Hannah Fleet, I hope you do!"

"What?!"

"You've got some serious baggage you're carrying around. I don't know what it is, and I don't even know if you know what it is—but I think you know what I mean."

Hannah exhaled. *Maybe this trip to see Allie will lead to some answers—or maybe more questions.* She inhaled deeply, holding the breath as she looked back to see the email from United fade into an updated screen saver: "Let go." Maudie's hands rested gently on her shoulders—warm, loving. Hannah let the breath go. Her eyes prickled with tears. *I'm going to London. I'm going to reconnect with my daughter. Life is good.*

CHAPTER 16

New Titles

JAMES

"Jim! Jimmy!" James held his breath, smiled, and turned to face his boss Dan. The last person to get away with calling him by his childhood name was Cal. "I bet you were Jimmy as a kid, weren't you?"

"Yes, Danny, I was." Dan bucked his chin back, but then laughed. "Got me there, Jimmy, I wasn't expecting that." Dan pulled James into his office. "Jim, I've got exciting news. Just picked up a client—big publishing house—in need of staffing a new division. You like books, don't you?"

"Love books—just spent my lunch hour at Cooke's" . . . selecting his next read from the Spirituality and New Science section. If anyone from work had seen him, he'd have turned towards Science Fiction. The juxtaposition of these sections amused him. He'd been raised in Christian Science, though he'd left it as a teenager.

His parents had met in college at a church fellowship meeting, the first time for both of them. It wasn't until they were married and Jimmy was twelve that they realized neither of them actually believed the doctrine—each attending only for the other. It took the heavy breath of death leaning over them to bring that to the surface. Fear drew them together as they joined hands to face it.

"Excellent! I knew you were my man for this. You don't mind relocating again?" It wasn't a question, rather a reminder of why he pulled in such a generous salary.

James wiggled his feet for assurance that they hadn't formed a strong attachment here. "Fine by me. I'm in a month-to-month rental—as always. When do I leave?"

"Two months. Big publishing event happening in the Bay Area, south of San Francisco in June. You'll have a few weeks before the event to meet with the head honchos to schedule interviews during the event. Marilyn will work out all the travel arrangements. I want you to wrap up your current assignments in the next few weeks so you can focus exclusively on this new client. Details later. For now, you're going to need to push to fill the Trans Media Q position. Found anyone yet?"

"I have a few leads, but it's a pretty eclectic skill set. Programming, customer service, and branding—really should be three positions, not one."

"They think they'll save money. I've tried to reason with the guy. He says it's the benefits packages that would kill him, not the salaries. I promised we'd give it a shot. See what you can do, Jim."

Back in his office, James gazed at the photo on the wall, mountains reflected in a still lake. In the thin strip of its glass frame a reflection of eyes looked back—James's or Jim's? Or Jimmy's? Once he'd left for college, James had left his childhood name behind, stepping into his given name as a portal to adulthood. But to Cal, he was only ever Jimmy. *New location, new assignment, new name. Why not? From Jimmy to James—now Jim. What the hell.*

A week later a small package arrived, containing a black and gold embossed name badge: "Jim Wescott, Publishing Specialist." He carried it into the kitchen. Dan and two co-workers were tearing into brown bags and take-out. Marilyn waited by the microwave for her lasagna. Jim flashed the badge at Dan. "Publishing Specialist?"

Dan smiled, swallowing a mouthful of submarine sandwich. "Yeah, forgot to mention I gave you a new title while I was talking with Imprint. They were really impressed that we had a Publishing Specialist. Cinched the deal. Hey, they're publishers—titles matter, right?" Dan laughed at his own joke and shifted to get a coffee refill. Marilyn had the pot in hand, anticipating his need as usual, and gave him a pour. "Thanks," he said, angling his next huge bite of sub. "Hey Marilyn, you can have a new title, too: Angel."

"No thanks. Halos aren't my style."

"What title would you prefer?" Gary asked.

"How about CEO?" They all laughed. "Clever Efficient Officer—help me out here, guys."

"Granted, you do deserve that," Dan agreed.

Marilyn grinned and pulled a book out of her purse. It caught Jim's eye.

"What are you reading?"

"*Reality is Not What It Seems*—about quantum physics."

"Reading quantum physics and you want to be CEO. I think I'd better watch out!" Marilyn rolled her eyes while the guys chuckled.

Jim, sandwich in hand, sat next to Marilyn, trying to read her book over her shoulder. She moved it over closer. "Better?"

"Thanks."

It described an experiment that proved that intentions can impact not only the future but also the past. "Wait—what? That's crazy." Marilyn looked at him questioningly. He pointed to the text. "There's actual scientific evidence we can change the past?"

He'd stopped reading to chew on the idea as well as the grilled veggie sandwich. *Could that really be true? How?* He let his mind slide down the familiar slope of the one day in his past he'd give anything to change.

Gary leaned over to Dan. "That's not physics, that's sci-fi." They laughed while Marilyn gave James a sideways look.

"You okay?" She tucked a bookmark in and set the book down.

"Hm? Yeah, yeah sure. I'm not really hungry." He left without looking at anyone in the room. Better to focus on work.

The Trans Media Q assignment was impossible—everyone knew it. Mind churning with ideas from the book, Jim closed his door, faced the window, and closed his eyes. He imagined the managers at Trans Media Q writing up the request for their super-human dream, then pictured the computer screen on which they typed the skill set requirements. Once that was clear, he imagined them backspacing through the words "customer service" and "branding." Leaving just "programming." His lips pulled into a smile.

"Jim!" Dan burst in. "What're you doing?"

"Nothing. Just needed to give my eyes a break from the screen. What do you need?"

"I just forwarded an email from Imprint. Setting up a management team call." He gave Jim a side-eye look. "You sure you're okay? Boyfriend trouble?"

"I'm not in a relationship. And I'm not—"

"Take it easy, just checking."

"I'm fine. I'll check email after I contact some programmers for Trans Media."

"Right. Don't forget customer service and branding." He rolled his eyes and left.

Jim stopped at Cooke's on his way home and purchased five books on quantum physics and consciousness research, including the book Marilyn was reading.

Shortly before bed he checked his email. One programmer had already responded—this woman was his top candidate, a perfect fit to handle the programmer part of the job for Trans Media. He was surprised to discover she had just completed a contract and was initiating the search for her next position when she'd received Jim's note. He leaned back into his pillow and pictured again the managers backspacing.

The next day Dan pounced on him as he arrived, bouncing like a kid who just won a trophy.

"Jim! It's your lucky day! You're not going to believe this!"

"Because I don't have lucky days?"

"Because Trans Media called. They say they reconsidered the job request, and they—"

"Wait—they only want the programmer." Jim interrupted.

"Yeah! No! I mean they want all three skills but in three separate people like we advised, but they prioritized the programmer. Did you talk to them yesterday, get them to see straight? I tied myself in knots trying to get through to them. What did you do?"

"Just some backspacing."

"Huh? What's that mean? 'Backspacing.' What're you talking about?"

"I didn't call them. Just things working out, I guess. I didn't mean anything." Not anything he could explain, anyway, and certainly not anything he thought Dan would buy as legit.

"You should take up gambling. You're one lucky guy!"

Jim returned to his office, a new believer in his own capacity to change his life. As if he'd stepped into a science fiction movie. He was a bit giddy—what else could he fix? What were the possibilities? What were the limits? His mind perused his childhood. He was in the hospital when he was nine, sweating, delirious. Something he'd eaten. In his flashes of lucidity he saw the fear in his parents, felt the pull of their love, their intent that he survive. Then he thought of Cal. No backspacing would bring him back. Imagining the bullet ripping backwards into the revolver that released it, blowing up the fucker who shot Cal. But mental revenge seemed beyond the possible.

Jim's eyes fell onto his book, remembering what the author and that woman at that library book sale had said about anger. He knew it was flat out destructive. Closing his eyes, he took a deep breath. The scent of spring flowers crept in gently. A deeper breath brought them in more assertively. His muscles eased.

Maybe reconnecting with my daughter . . . He took a deep breath and let it out slowly. Closing his eyes, he said the words internally and then again aloud. "I intend to reconnect with my daughter, for her to see who I am, not just who she thinks I was."

As he reopened his eyes, excitement tiptoed back into the room. He set those thoughts aside and focused on tasks at hand.

The programmer was the right candidate, he was certain. "I need to call her. Then I just have to convince Trans Media." He stopped the thought like pulling the emergency brake on a train. "No. I don't have to convince anyone. If it's right, they'll choose her. If not, I'll keep searching for the person who's supposed to be in that job." *Things are looking up. Definitely looking up.*

CHAPTER 17

Conscious Authorship

HANNAH

Hannah settled into a cozy chair in the travel section of her favorite bookstore cafe on Filmore Street to study up on London. Mag's Mugs had become her favorite spot to consume the tantalizing array of used books, beverages, and bakery treats. She appreciated their pastries, the homey atmosphere of the comfy chairs and reading lamps, the tall stacks of books scattered about like in her childhood bedroom, daring you to pull one from the bottom, like playing Jenga. A great spot to spend her birthday. As she set down her chai latte and muffin, a woman squeezed past, knocking a book off the stack beside Hannah.

"Sorry." She handed it to Hannah.

"No problem." Hannah smiled, her eyes sliding over the plain cover. A gold "H" embossed in the corner snared her attention. She opened it. The first page had just four words: "She turned the page." And so she did.

"She'd caught the joke of the opening sentence and had been amused. Mildly. The muscles around her mouth tugged lightly toward a smile." Exactly what Hannah was doing. Words mirroring her present inserted a question mark on her statement of reality. Her mind peeked back at the previous page. If she turned back, the words would be true yet again. *It's a literary hall of mirrors!* She read on.

"But a new uneasiness set in: would a story unfold? Or would this sense of observing herself offset on the page—like a shadow that can't keep up with its creator—persist?" *Ridiculous sentence,* but she was entranced. "She set the book down, uncertain whether to continue." Hannah lay the book in her lap.

The worn leather cover must have lived in an old attic. Her fingers glided across the "H" like deciphering a childhood memory in Braille.

Four decades ago, her friend Danielle had invited Hannah along to visit her grandparents. They let the girls explore the attic, a dusty rough-hewn cave filled with curiosities: a cigar box full of skeleton keys, a child-size rocking chair with broken cane seat, a steamer trunk protecting a wedding dress and lacy baby clothes. Stacks of leather-bound books that smelled of history and mystery nurtured her imagination and incited Hannah's desire to become an author. Brittle yellowed pages under Danielle's flashlight revealed treasure maps of poetry and prose. The light brushed over a leather cover with a gold embossed "H" just like this one.

Hannah had picked it up reverently. Danielle had found a treasure too, a small music box. "Let's say a prayer," Danielle had said suddenly, sitting on a dusty bench.

"A what?"

"Whenever I want something, I say a prayer." Hannah clearly didn't understand. "I ask God for what I want."

"Does it work?" Hannah's parents had never talked about prayer, and her experience with asking for things usually produced the opposite. But she really wanted this book. She sat next to her friend.

"Sometimes. Close your eyes. Dear God, please can I have this music box? Okay, your turn."

"Dear God, please can I have this book?" They opened their eyes.

"Let's go ask Grandpa."

Too afraid to ask if she could have the book, she'd summoned up the courage to ask to borrow it. Danielle's grandfather seemed delighted and gave it to her to keep. Hannah remembered the feeling well. *I felt like a fountain of soda, all bubbly and light. The ancient book was hands down the best present I'd ever received.* Danielle insisted her prayer had been answered. She was so excited she made the mistake of showing it to her parents.

"Danielle showed me how to pray and I asked God for it and then her grandpa gave it to me."

Her father scowled. "Take it back. You can't keep it."

Mom had looked sympathetic. "It's her birthday, maybe he—"

"We don't even know this guy. He shouldn't be giving a seven-year-old presents. It's dangerous."

"Eight," Hannah had mumbled.

"What did you say?"

"I'm eight now."

"Whatever. Take it back. And I don't want to hear another word about prayer. We're atheists. There is no God."

The next day Danielle made her an offer. "I know what. I'll keep it in my room. You can come over and read it any time you want." Her visits to Danielle's had increased after that, especially because she'd recognized Danielle as a loyal friend.

Hannah now ran her hand over the book in her lap. *Are the words mirroring or mocking?* Questions gathered like ingredients in the mixing bowl of her mind: *What is the past I've been so desperate to remember? Does it have any substance? What about the future? Can it be more than a thought now? Is there any gap between the past and the future? Or is everything really "just now" and that's all there is?* She worked the questions like pastry dough, careful not to overwork them, then she set them aside to rest.

Hannah lifted her gaze to the café. She felt connected to it— part of it.

"Hi Hannah! Not used to seeing you in this section."

Hannah smiled up at the store clerk. "Hey Tina, I'm going to London in July. Figured I should do some research."

"Cool! I've always wanted to go. Lots of great titles to choose from in this section. And here . . . we're giving away bookmarks today."

"Thanks, Tina." Hannah read the message. "Enjoy Now—it's all there is." She burst out laughing.

"What's funny?"

She flashed Tina the bookmark.

"My life. Everything. Hey, question for you: if Now is really all there is, then what was yesterday? And last week? And our entire past?"

"Yeah, well. I guess they're just different versions of Now. But they're not Now anymore." Tina pulled up an upholstered footstool. "So maybe I should forgive my boyfriend for being such a jerk last night. He was *such* a jerk. But Now, I guess, it's just a story I'm telling myself—and everyone else—so I can stay mad at him."

"Hm."

"I think I'll forgive him," she said with happy determination. "I should keep circulating. See you later."

"Wait, sit down, there is no later, remember?"

"Oooo, you're right." She plopped down again.

"Hey, did you ever see *What the Bleep Do We Know?*"

"Nope. Don't think so."

"I watched it with my friend Maudie the other night. It's about quantum physics."

"Oh my God, did you stay awake through it?"

"It was weirdly awesome. There's this scientist who says the mind can't tell the difference between our thoughts and what's out there in physical reality."

"Wait, what? Are you saying that I can't tell the difference between the stud of a boyfriend I wish I had and the one I've actually got? Not buying it."

"Not quite. More like if you imagine running a race in your mind, your body and brain are behaving as if you're actually running the race."

"Sounds like a great way to convince myself I don't need to go to the gym. I can just sit in bed and imagine it."

"A whole new way to experience mental gymnastics," Hannah laughed.

"But in a way, I get it. I mean, if I focus on my boyfriend being a jerk, I'm making it my experience Now."

"Yeah. And when I dream about my trip to London that's where I am—for the moment. At least until I go back to focusing on what's in front of me."

"Like those Escher drawings—perfectly logical and completely impossible at the same time. Okay I really need to move it or in my not-yet-existent future Now I could be out of a job. See ya!"

Looking around at the books surrounding her, Hannah realized she'd been going through life as if she had no control over the story that was unfolding as her life. *What if I consciously author my life? Treat myself as a character in my own novel. Or autobiography—but looking ahead to the future instead of back at the past.*

She'd grown up believing that life was a process of coping with whatever misfortunes and obstacles happened her way. Occasionally good stuff happened, too—but life was more about dealing with all the crap. *What would it mean to take responsibility for all that I've created?* Having to take responsibility for her entire past didn't seem fair. *Surely there's some formula for co-creation.* Freeing her father of blame for abusing her didn't seem right. But giving him attention now when he's long dead, letting him dominate *this* moment wasn't right either. *I can choose to accept it all and still make up a new story, start over—now—and keep starting over continuously.*

Her heart was racing—maybe something in the chai, or maybe the banana nut muffin came from one of those medicinal marijuana places. Hannah was feeling light-headed. Her eyes slid over the bookshelves displaying spines and grabbed a title out of the mass: *IF.* She wrote it in her journal. Another title jumped out at her: *YOU.* She added it. To the left, another single word title:

BELIEVE! It was like some kind of life-size Ouiji board.

A man in his forties in khaki cargo pants and a hoodie wandered in. Perusing spines, he squatted down to check the bottom shelf. The back of his blue sweatshirt broadcast: ANYthing is Possible.

"Holy shit," she breathed.

He turned. His handsome face looked quizzical. "Never really thought of shit as holy. But hell—why not? Releasing what is no longer needed is kind of a sacred practice, I guess." He smiled at her. "I'll bet that's not what you meant." Then he looked serious. "You okay?"

"Anything is possible," she said.

He laughed. "Yeah, I guess so."

"I was just quoting the back of your shirt: 'Anything is possible.' I didn't mean about shit being holy."

"Oh. Found it in the bottom of my drawer—haven't worn it since I can't remember when. It says that?"

Hannah pulled out her cell phone. "Turn around, I'll show you." She snapped a picture of his back.

"Cool. Thanks. Hey, could you text me that?"

"What, the message?"

"The picture. I can tell you the number."

"It's *your* shirt. Is this some creepy way to get my phone number?"

"No! Forget it, I was just—forget it." He turned away and started to leave the Spirituality section.

"I'm sorry. I didn't mean that you are creepy or anything, I'm having—or *was* having a really—wait, how could you not know what your shirt says?"

The young man with sandy colored hair looked embarrassed. "You probably don't want to know."

"Actually, I really do." He looked uncertain, "I'm a writer. We like to know weird stuff. Not that it's weird, whatever it is."

"I think it's weird."

"Okay, then maybe it is. But weird is cool."

"I do the first part of my day—you know, getting up, dressing, all that stuff—with my eyes closed, as if I were blind."

"Wow, that is weird."

"Thanks."

"Just agreeing with you. Why? Why do you pretend to be blind?"

"My brother was. Not like I want to be blind, but just to share his experience."

"'*Was.*' Like Amazing Grace? Like he was blind, but now can see? Or *was* like . . ." she trailed off. "I'm sorry. None of my business."

A moment passed. "A writer, huh? What do you write? Are you published?"

She paused. "I'm sorry. This is really awkward with me sitting and talking up at you. I'm thinking we should decide if we're actually going to have this conversation that I started so rudely, or if we should pretend it never happened and I should let you go find whatever you're looking for and go back to my—" Hannah glanced back down at her notebook—*IF YOU BELIEVE!* "—my *Bruce Almighty* moment. You know, messages from God everywhere you turn."

"Love that flick—Morgan Freeman as God."

"Right? He's my favorite. And Bruce with the 'Give me a sign!' moment—"

"And the truck loaded with signs pulls in front of him."

"And he still doesn't get it."

"Yeah." He walked over to a double stack of large books on the floor about the height of a stool and took a couple books off one to even them out to sit eye level with Hannah. "I'm Tigue. That's what my family calls me. I think it was actually 'cause I always wore my mother out: like 'Fa-Tigue.' My real name is Wendell, but Tigue stuck."

Hanna smiled. "Hannah. My father's idea, I think." She imitated her drunken father slurring his words: 'Hannanuf.' He used to yell at Mom, 'I hanna nuffuh you!' I thought he was talking about me."

Tigue didn't know what to say and held up a nearby book: *When "I'm Sorry" Isn't Enough*. Hannah pulled a book from the shelf in front of her: *Moving On*. Awkward silence. As if their train had pulled into a station and they weren't sure if they were supposed to get off or not.

"It wasn't an Amazing Grace thing."

"I'm sorry."

Tigue looked at the journal in her lap. "So, do you?"

"Do I . . . what?"

He pointed at the three words in caps.

"Well, everyone believes something. Figuring out what that *is* is the challenge." Tigue turned around to show her the back of his shirt again. "Oh. That." He settled again on the wobbly pile. His gaze and silence both made Hannah uncomfortable. She gulped her chai and stuffed some muffin in her mouth. His gaze did not let up, so she shrugged. "Do you?"

"Why are you here?" He leaned back against the shelves behind him.

Hannah's eyes looked side to side. "You mean here in Mag's? Or here—like *here*. Like in this body on this planet here?"

"Whichever."

Hannah suddenly leaned forward. "Do you believe we can write our own life story? I don't mean an autobiography where you're just writing about the past. I mean like—create our own lives?"

"Sure. Don't you?"

"Not sure yet. I grew up with the mantra 'tough shit—this is what you get.' I don't really like the idea that I created that, because I hated it."

"Well, it's not like we create it all by ourselves. Seems like it's more of a group project—a team sport."

Hannah sat back. "I hated group projects at school."

"I think it's like an experiment teachers do to find out how kids handle getting pissed off at their friends."

"My partners always ditched me, leaving me to do all the work."

A buzzing caused Tigue to dig in his pocket. He looked at his phone. "Shoot. I have to take this. And I'm way late. See you around." *ANYthing is Possible* flashed by Hannah as Tigue swiped the screen, talking as he left the store. "I'm on my way. I'm sorry but I got . . ." The shop door banged.

She picked up the brown leather book in her lap. Flipping it over, she opened to the last page: "It felt to her in the moment like an ending, but something in her sensed it was actually a beginning. A thought had taken root and was already beginning to sprout. Her story was about to change, not because the puppeteer had rewritten the script, but because she saw that the strings were as imaginary as the puppeteer. The pen was in her hand, the blank page open before her. She closed the book and started the new chapter."

Hannah closed the book. As she set it aside, a thin pen slipped out and dropped in her lap.

CHAPTER 18

Revisions

The summer fog had cleared early, revealing a classic California sky. Signs for Publishing Expo West dominated the area surrounding the Hyatt Regency. Jim had flown in a week early to get reoriented and do the first round of interviews for the management level positions in the two days leading up to the Expo. All that remained was a junior acquisitions position and keeping an eye out for possible interns.

He set up chairs on either side of a table in a small meeting room near the registration area. He tested them for comfort and stability to help interviewees get past the "all nerves" part of the process. A pitcher of ice water and glasses sat ready. The packed schedule meant not much break time, and the last two interview slots were empty, so he might get out early. He and the HR team at Imprint had already vetted the scheduled candidates for skills and experience. There were no stand-out applicants for the position he was aiming to fill today, at least not in terms of experience. Disappointing, but maybe he'd find a gem yet. His job was to ferret out the person who would best fit the team—right attitude, good communication, enthusiasm, and energy.

He smoothed the necktie he'd purchased before his move, a bold image of colorful books in tasteful contrast to his light blue shirt. He'd made a statement not just with the choice of ties, but by buying it at the family-owned Cooke's, not Amazon (who also happened to be a competitor to his new client). The assembling crowd murmured in the Grand Peninsula Foyer.

There was something charged about this moment—an energy, pulling him forward, though he couldn't fathom toward what. With his name badge touting his new title and new name—he'd given up on his boss calling him James—and the drastic change from a lifetime of thick hair and beard all lent to the feeling of starting fresh.

He let his eyes travel again down the list of candidates. The empty boxes at the end drew his attention.

Jim checked the time—enough to find some coffee or chai before the first interview. The air conditioning was blasting, as he'd expected. He reached for his dark blue jacket, neatly hung over the back of a chair away from the table, then stopped—the air or something had changed. Not the physical air, but . . . He couldn't understand his own thought: *What other kind of air is there? It's more like atmosphere than air.* He thought of force fields from old *Star Trek* episodes—Captain Kirk walking into a wall and falling backward. *Just my imagination.* He hummed the Temptations' "Just My Imagination" as he turned toward the door.

Registration was at the far side of the spacious lobby. Hannah tried to get her bearings, smoothing her windblown hair and joining the growing crowd of people waiting in the A-L line. Even in her best outfit, she felt underdressed among the throng of stylish professionals toting large bags and satchels heavy with manuscripts seeking discovery or representation. *What stories are hatching inside?* She adjusted the strap of her shoulder bag bulging with two copies of her best seller, ten resumes, and the stash of business cards Jaz had helped her print.

The tall woman in line in front of her wore a fitted maroon jacket and skirt, with purse to match and gold-trimmed, insanely high heels. Hannah's eyes flitted back and forth between the two, trying to figure out if they had been sold as matching accessories or if this woman was just an amazing shopper. She hypothesized that Ms. Tailored Suit breathed thinner air up there. Hannah's view of the woman's shoulder blades made her feel small. They were unlikely to ever meet in a clothing store. Hannah had to remind herself that used clothing was her environmental choice.

She looked at her own Mary Janes and raised her shoulders competitively. Her thin, cream-colored sweater had been one of her better finds a week ago, but she sniffed the underarms each morning to make sure it really did smell okay. She restrained herself from checking again. She needed to lighten up here, appreciate the collegial atmosphere.

The lines spread out, blocking any view of the registration table as old acquaintances met and chatted ahead of her. She caught the eye of a nice-looking man in the M-Z line. They smiled. He tried to peer through the backs of the people in front of him. "This is for registration, right?" he asked Hannah.

"Yes. But if it were a buffet we might starve. There are only a couple people working the table."

"You an author?"

"Yes. You?"

"Larry Finnegan. Editor mostly. I write a bit but have only self-published. And just once."

"I think they call it independent publishing now, don't they? I mean, at least that's what I heard at a BAIPA meeting."

"BAIPA?"

"Bay Area Independent Publishers Association. The Bay Area is leading the pack in independent publishing they say. Who knows? Statistics are not my thing."

"Oh." He nodded in a way that made Hannah feel like a lame tour guide.

"I didn't verify the info. Or the source. Just a . . . whatever." Sliding deeper into lameness, she threw out a line to save herself. "Did you say Finnegan?"

"Yes. What's your name?"

"Hannah. Hannah Fleet."

"Nice necklace by the way."

"Thank you." Hannah's hand went to the delicate silver necklace her grandmother had given her on the last birthday they celebrated together. "Sorry to break this to you, but—you're in the wrong line. That's the M to Z line. This is A to L."

"Oh. Thanks. Hard to tell where the lines are." He looked way back to the end of Hannah's line. "Well, I guess . . ."

Hannah looked around. No one seemed to be paying much attention to the fact of lines. "You can just join me, I guess. I mean, you were here before they were anyway." Made sense and she figured no one would notice anyway. If someone complained, Finnegan could explain himself.

He appeared to be caught in a moral dilemma. The two women behind Hannah were hotly debating the intimate details of misplaced commas and paying no attention to the misplaced editor. "Okay. Thanks." He took a step closer to Hannah, smiled a bit awkwardly. "You staying in one of the local hotels?"

"I live in San Francisco."

"Lucky you."

"Thanks. But I've given up believing in luck."

His awkward smile again. "Guess I should have figured that out—that you live here." He responded to her quizzical look, "Bay Area something Publishers, whatever that was."

Hannah nodded, relieved that it wasn't her comment about luck that gave her away. Although why it might matter, she didn't know. A residue of her neurotic need to be anonymous. For so many years disappearing had been her strategy for survival. *When will I lay that pack down and walk away?* Jaz had asked her that just yesterday. *She'd made it sound so easy. But if I set it down and walk away from this personality, TSA would probably track me down and arrest me for abandoning a loaded device.*

"Nice city. My first time here, so I played tourist yesterday."
He shuffled forward with Hannah as the line progressed half a
human forward.

"What did you see? There's too much to do the whole city in
a day."

"Cable car, Ghiradelli Square, Fisherman's Wharf. I saw the
Golden Gate Bridge but didn't have time to walk it. No tickets
available for Alcatraz, so I went to Golden Gate Park."

"I love the park. Riding through and visiting buffalo."

Larry screwed up his face. "Buffalo?"

Hannah smiled. "I guess you missed them."

"I'm from Buffalo—New York. Funny!"

"Synchronous," Hannah mumbled into the general hubbub.

Larry dug into his bag, jiggling and adjusting its contents
to extricate a book. He held up a paperback entitled "Buffalo
Tails," the cover exposing the backside of a buffalo studying a
sign for the town. "If only I'd seen them. I could have added
a California chapter and still stayed true to the title. Maybe
I'll extend my visit." Hannah chuckled in spite of herself. His
obvious pleasure was contagious. They shuffled forward to
second in line.

"Almost there," she said. *Should I offer to let him go first
or just step forward? Maybe just wait to see what he does?*
Such social rules were easier back when men opened doors
for women and held their chairs. Now it was just weird and
confusing—though she loved when people did that for each
other, except when motivated by gender assumptions about
the poor, weak woman.

"Next?" The woman behind the desk looked between Hannah
and Larry.

Larry glanced at Hannah for a signal. "After you. I'm the
interloper."

Hannah got through registration as quickly as possible and
smiled kindly at Larry as she walked away—enough to be polite

but without giving any message that she hoped to continue the conversation. She chided herself. She had recently decided—with some nudging from Jaz—to make an effort to re-enter the world of dating. Conversation with Larry was a reminder of how awkward early dates can be.

The wide, open corridor that led to restaurants and shops skirted the Grand Peninsula Foyer. The registration area was churning with anticipation. Two irregular lines spread across the space, tethered at one end by the registration table, swaying in the winds of interaction like the tails of a kite. From even this slightly raised perspective, Jim could see patterns emerge. Around the perimeter, loners clung to the safety of walls, studying conference pamphlets, observing eyes taking it all in, electrons encircling the nucleus of energy.

Jim ordered his drink and watched the hubbub as he waited. A woman with golden hair was moving away from the registration table and seemed undecided about whether to join the perimeter or stay in the nucleus. His drink ready, Jim turned to the self-serve corner to add an extra sprinkle of cinnamon to his chai.

Taking a deep breath, Hannah pulled the conference schedule out of her canvas bag and checked the time. She felt butterflies about her job interview, even though there were hours before her appointment. It was the last slot of the day, the only available one left by the time she got up the courage to apply. By then the interviewer would likely be too tired to listen or care. She wasn't even sure the interview was confirmed, since she hadn't received a confirmation email. Uncertain whether to go confirm the appointment, she looked at the conference map to locate the interview room. Summoning up her courage, she moved through the crowd in that direction.

The room was empty when she arrived. It appeared to be set up and ready, but there was no schedule posted for her to check. Letting go another long breath, she headed toward the room where the keynote address would be starting soon. As she walked back down the steps to join the slow movement toward the main hall, she noticed a man walking in the direction of the room she'd just left and wondered if he was the interviewer. He walked with confidence and ease, eyes on his phone, cup in hand. Her arms tingled, goose bumps rising.

Someone bumped her. "Sorry—oh, it's you again. Hi. Crowded." Larry Finnegan was beside her.

"It is. Got registered okay then?"

He patted his conference bag. "All set. Shall we sit together? For the keynote?"

"Sure. That would be nice." They shuffled forward in companionable silence.

There were two morning sessions with several track options for each time frame. For the first they split up, then bumped into each other again and were both planning to attend the same workshop next. Lunch followed and it seemed logical to sit together as they had each brought a bag lunch. They found an outdoor seating area where dozens of others also gathered around food while conversing, building friendships. Hannah was glad to not be alone.

After the final morning interview, Jim realized the line for the restaurant was too long to afford him time to eat there, so he picked up a grab-and-go lunch at the 3Sixty Market and headed out for some fresh air. He felt restless. After sitting for hours, he decided to walk. He passed an area with several folks eating and noticed again the woman with golden hair. Her back was to him, so he couldn't see her face. She was with a man, perhaps her partner. Hard to tell at events like this. But he didn't recall the man being with her when he saw her earlier in the Foyer. The man looked up and caught Jim's eyes. They nodded to each other, and Jim walked on.

By the end of the afternoon, Jim was beat. The candidates had been lackluster, the empty interview slots remained empty. He felt frustrated, thought back to the morning and the feeling that something important would happen today. So much for trusting feelings.

As he checked the room for anything he might have not packed up and was about to grab his jacket with his name badge, a text came in from his HR contact at Imprint. "One more today." As the dots indicated a follow up text was in the works, his phone died.

"Shit." He set his stuff down and pulled out his laptop, hoping they would have emailed as well. But he'd left his computer unplugged all day, and that too blacked out. The charger was in the car.

As Jim whisked into the doorway, Hannah was poised to poke her head inside. Their heads came within inches, sending them each into reverse, both talking at once: "Oh! Sorry!"

"I didn't see—"

"No, I'm—"

"Really—" Their simultaneous apologies quickly trailed off as their eyes met. *The woman with golden hair—that familiar golden hair.*

Hannah dropped her eyes to the floor then at the interview table, not sure if this was her competition or—hopefully not—the interviewer. Her hand went unconsciously to brush back her hair.

The gesture, like an old friend's out of context, startled Jim. A scent awakened a subtle yearning. "I'm sorry. I should have been looking where I was going." The voice surrounded Hannah like fuzzy bedroom slippers. "Did you . . . Are you . . . ? I mean . . . What do I mean?" He smiled, rolled his eyes.

Hannah felt like she'd lost her place reading—had looked up, then down into a different book—one she'd read so long ago she didn't recall the plot or characters. She blinked several times, wiping the windshield in hopes of a clearer view. Jim smiled and the sun emerged to light her way. "I have an interview scheduled—at least I think it was scheduled, but I never got a confirmation and I'm hoping—you know—" She looked behind her to see if any other candidates were waiting.

"Yes." They stood a moment before Jim shook himself into action. "Come in. I was going to get my computer charger, but—"

"Please go ahead, it's okay. I can wait."

"No need. Anymore."

"Oh. Okay."

"I'm . . ." She didn't recognize him, he realized, but he felt certain it was her. He proceeded with caution. ". . . I'm . . ." He waved vaguely toward the interview table. ". . . doing the interviews."

He covered his handsome face with his hands. His tan spoke of time outdoors. Hannah noticed two knuckles on his left hand were scraped and healing. When she looked up at him, she saw a light in his brown eyes, his smile crinkling them at the corners. The image reflected back to her showed a face prettier than the way she saw herself. "Should I sit?"

He looked around as if he was new to the space and didn't trust any of the chairs. "You know, I could really use a cup of something hot. Can I treat you? Least I can do for nearly running you down."

"That would be great actually. I planned to book the first interview so I could get it over and not have to stress all day, but this was the only time left. I'm good at stressing. Oh, shoot. That's not the kind of thing to say in an interview, is it? I can *handle* stress—I mean, I have lots of practice, but . . ." She squeezed her eyes closed. "I should shut up now."

"I'm not taking notes," Jim reassured her. "Shall we?" They walked toward the conference center lobby.

"But it's not like you're going to forget what I said, and . . . I *really* think I should shut up now."

"I promise not to hold anything against you." But Hannah wished he would hold something against her, hardly recognizing the feeling because it had been so long. His arms looked strong, his smile warm. She was starting to think she had slipped and fallen into a romance novel. They skirted the sunken lobby area still abuzz with chatting professionals, though the crowd was starting to thin. Along the other side of the fray, they found a coffee shop. "What's your beverage of choice?"

"Chai latte with almond milk please."

Jim ordered two and passed one to Hannah.

"Thanks." They found a table near the window with a view of the diminishing hubbub, but away from its noise.

"Just before we bumped into each other—literally—I'd gotten a text that there was another appointment, but I didn't get the name."

"Hannah." She held up her name tag. "Sorry, I hate wearing these."

"Hannah," he repeated.

"Hannah Fleet."

"Hannah. It's me. Jim. I mean James. Wescott."

The two sat looking at each other, their eyes playing over each other's features, finding the remnants of their younger selves.

Hannah leaned back. "Oh my God. I can't believe it. You look . . . so different . . . really good. Not that you didn't look good before, but—"

"So do you. I got rid of a lot of hair. And a lot of other stuff too. Less visible stuff. And I go by Jim now."

They stared at their steaming cups of chai as recognition

settled in and took its place at the table. It sat quietly, without assumption or demand or turmoil, more like the tea—warming and comforting.

"You look really different with short hair," Hannah ventured, "and no beard!"

They shared a smile. "And you look, wow, so much more at peace. It's good. Really good." A light of connection flashed across his face. "I think I . . . Wait, did you have a book signing in Princeton back in . . . Oh, gosh, when was that?"

"Last November. You were there?" She didn't remember him in the audience.

"I missed it, actually. Sorry. I didn't even know it was happening until I walked in. You'd already left."

She grinned. "Synchronicity. Or maybe almost but not quite. Still . . ."

Jim swirled his cup, the chai reclaiming residual foam around the edges. "I barely knew the meaning of that word until sometime last year. But it seems to keep swimming around my pond these days. At first, I wasn't buying this whole thing like the law of attraction stuff—you've heard of that, right?" Hannah nodded. "I thought it was just woo-woo New Age, yeah—right—what drugs are you on?' But turns out the science is the real deal." He paused and smiled self-consciously. "Sorry. I haven't found anyone to talk to about this, but I find it really exciting." He recalled Phil's exuberance from about a year ago and understood.

"Me too." She sipped her chai, then set it down gently on the table between them. "How long have you worked for Imprint Digital? Got any insider tips for me?"

"Just started. Only a consultant—not really an insider. Sorry, I'm not much help."

"I guess that question was probably—"

"It was fine. I would happily tell you everything I know about them, but so far I've only been briefed on what they're looking for in someone to add to the acquisitions team. 'A junior position with great growth potential.' Which means the pay is lacking. But it's a great company from what I can tell. Very team oriented. It's less about skills—they plan to train anyway. More about making sure the new person belongs on the Imprint Digital bus, so to speak."

"Bus? Not sure I follow."

"Attitude, communication, energy, personality, teamwork, able to both lead and follow, persistence—skills that may take longer to develop and require a concerted effort. Think of the company as the bus, the employees the travelers. They need to get along well together, even in tight spaces on long trips—or it can be hell on the company culture. Less important initially to get people into the right seats on the bus—or positions within the company—than to make sure they are a fit overall."

"That makes sense. Never thought about that." They sipped in unison, neither inclined to try to go back in time or to sort out their shared history.

"Yours is a cookbook, right?"

"Yes."

"So, what's your favorite recipe?"

"Depends what I'm in the mood for. But hard to imagine ever saying no to a Coconut Dream."

"What's that?"

"Cookie. A cakey square, like a brownie." She peered over her mug at him. "Great with tea. I wish I'd brought some. You like coconut?"

"With chocolate?"

"Naturally."

"One of my favorite combos. I wonder if I've had those before. Coconut Dreams rings a bell."

"We served them at the signing. But they disappeared pretty quickly. They were gone well before I had to leave."

"I remember seeing chocolate crumbs. Man, it poured that night!"

"I was drenched just getting into the taxi." Hannah's hair slipped forward. She pushed it back.

"That was you! Wasn't it? As I was about to go in, a woman ran out and ducked into a taxi. That must have been you!"

"Oh my gosh! Yeah, it must have been."

"Your hair caught the light from the shop windows. Golden." Hannah brushed another lock of hair behind her ear. "Beautiful."

"Thank you."

"We must've just missed each other. Amazing. But now here we are." They gazed at each other, smiling. A tremblor ran through Jim. "I guess I should ask you some questions."

Hannah stood, pulled her bag off the back of the chair. She felt a hand on hers. "Let's stay here," he said softly. "We don't have to be in that sterile room. Let's . . . enjoy our chai—and talk. Okay? I mean, unless you'd rather . . ."

"No. This is great. Really great." She resettled.

"I can order us refills."

"Sure."

"Back in a moment."

Hannah watched him. His movements, his smile, his manner—warmth wrapping her like a cashmere sweater.

Jim slipped back into his seat. "They'll bring it. So, tell me what you most love about the publishing world."

Hannah's eyes closed briefly as the scent of cinnamon and nutmeg morphed into the warm smell of old leather as she imagined the volumes that populated her life with their stories. "I love books."

"I remember that."

"I love how we can be in one place here and now. But all we have to do is open a book for a whole different world to engulf us. Or with nonfiction, how new ways of thinking erupt like magic. It's like—it's like Spring."

"Spring? How so?"

"When I was a kid, on the first warm day, Mom and I would

open all the windows and doors to blow the stale air out. I loved that—all those smells of closed-up living, gone. And how the smell of flowers drifted in. Like hope and possibility, something fresh that hadn't been there before. That's what great books do—they open all the windows and doors inside us, in our mind and our heart and our spirit. Then anything is possible. I mean, sometimes it feels like this world is looking for ways to beat us down—at least, that's what I used to think. But books! Books are like magic carpets, keys to a kingdom. They free us. You know? When I was a kid, books saved me—they literally saved me from so much crap . . ." They both sipped their tea. "Who I was is not who I am now." Hannah stopped, took a breath and released it slowly.

To Jim, she was like that fresh breeze blowing through him. Her scent reminded him of his grandmother's kitchen filled with the smell of baking pies. "Same here."

Fresh cups of chai arrived. Hannah took a sip, savoring its spicy heat as it rolled over her tongue. She waited for the next question. But Jim was silent, so she jumped back in.

"See, the way I look at it, books are not only opening up new worlds, they're also changing this world that we call the 'real world' because they change *us*. That's what I love about publishing. People really need books, more than most of us even realize. I like being part of that, even if it's only developing recipes."

"Don't go knocking recipes. Food is about as important as you can get. I can't imagine life without cookies, for example. Can you?"

Hannah grinned. "It would hardly be worth living."

"And what do you like least about publishing?"

"Is that a trick question?" Hannah looked askance at him.

"Nope. What *don't* you like about it?"

"That so many great manuscripts never make it into print. And that so many books never get read by the people that most need them. That's sad."

"What would you do about that?"

Hannah thought a moment. "Do my best to offer a way forward

for authors. Indie publishing is growing, and Imprint is an actual publisher, so maybe I shouldn't be saying this—but I am all for indie publishing. So if I'm in acquisitions and a book is rejected but I think it has something to offer the world, I'd encourage the author to publish on their own. I would. And I really want this job with Imprint Digital, so I'm hoping you can just ignore that if it's not what they would want to hear." She fingered the silver pencil charms on her necklace.

Jim stared at the necklace, transfixed, making her self-conscious. "That necklace . . ."

"Do you remember it? My grandmother commissioned it from a local artist in Kingston when I was nineteen. Means a lot to me."

"It's . . . lovely." It was a perfect match to the one Sammo had found in the bathroom in San Rafael when helping him pack for his move to Princeton. "Did you ever live in San Rafael?"

The question seemed innocuous but odd. It knocked her off kilter.

"Why do you ask?"

"No reason. Sorry." He stirred his tea. "Feels sometimes like life is a big puzzle I'm trying to solve."

"I know what you mean."

"What's the most stressful situation you've had to face, and how'd you deal with it?"

Not a question she'd expected. But she'd already made all those comments about stress earlier. *Maybe it's a question of my own devising.* "Well, the one that immediately comes to mind . . ." *Is not one I'm sure I want to share, might cost me this opportunity. But there it is, daring to be revealed.* She started hesitantly. "It wasn't a work thing."

"That's fine. We all have stressful stuff happen—we both know that. I know I haven't always handled it well." He studied his chai, Hannah studying him. "We're all just doing our best at any given moment." He looked up at her and they looked steadily at each other.

She nodded. "Yeah. I believe that."

Hannah gathered her thoughts. In the pause, Jim traced loose threads of memories back twenty-four years to the last time he'd seen Hannah—a time filled with stress and poor judgement.

"Well, I . . . got lost. Sort of."

Jim nodded thoughtfully, himself lost and tangled in a memory of a toddler with strawberry curls. He brought himself back to the present. "Lost . . . while traveling? Or . . . ?"

"Not exactly. I was on my bike and . . . it's kind of hard to explain."

"You bike? Cool. Me too." His smile was reassuring.

"I don't know what happened to me. It's like I fell out of the life I was living and landed in some alternate version of it. I couldn't remember anything from after . . . from after the Big Decision . . . that point when we had to decide about . . . about whether to abort . . . or have the baby. Allison."

Their eyes met briefly but both looked down immediately. Jim let his hand gently rest on hers. She didn't withdraw, but he didn't let it linger there.

"I felt like I lost myself. It was like I . . . it was like everything . . . disappeared. And I had to find it again. I had to find everything that was important . . . and figure out how to leave behind whatever wasn't . . . stuff that really doesn't matter anymore . . . or maybe never did. I thought maybe I'd lost my mind. But I hadn't! I did not lose my mind. Or if I did, I found it again and it's working really well. I want to be really super clear on that point."

Jim smiled. "You're coming through very clear now."

"Good. Anyway, whatever happened, I dealt with it by going forward, one step at a time, one day at a time. Staying in the Now. Figuring it out."

"And how did you figure it out?"

Hannah pictured her mental gratitude board with Maudie's and Jaz's names in bold colors and exclamation points. "I met two amazing women. They've been like family—but a better version of family than I grew up with. They've helped me shift the way I see things. When I'm uncertain making a decision, I bounce it off one of them. I'm so grateful for them. I've only ever told those women about getting lost. And now you."

"I'm honored. Thank you. Sounds like they're a great team for you."

"The best."

"It takes a lot of strength to be vulnerable. What happens when you disagree with them?"

"To be honest, I used to get defensive. Before I'd learned to trust them. Now I try to set my own ideas aside and try on theirs—like buying a pair of shoes. It's not always easy, but it brings out my Cinderella. I think it helps me make better decisions."

"What's your biggest goal?"

"Oh my gosh. For a while it was figuring out my past—until it no longer mattered. Now getting a job." She looked at him hopefully.

Jim pushed his cup to the center of the table. "Would you excuse me a minute? I'll be right back."

"Oh, sure, of course." Hannah watched as he walked right past the rest room and kept going. The cafe was sparsely occupied. Most of the attendees would be in the main hall now for the final keynote address.

James—in San Rafael. Her mind ricocheted between her own youth, Allie, James, and the journal she'd found, trying to piece together her own puzzle. But it was as if two puzzles were jumbled together and refused to match up. She took a deep breath, letting go of needing to understand, and refocusing on the interview. *How I blathered on! Have I totally ruined my chance at this job?*

She checked the time—the time frame for interviews was technically over. Minutes passed. *Is he coming back?* Her uncertainty increased as time ticked by. *Should I wait? Find him in the interview room? Go home?*

By the time her chai was cold, Hannah had reconstructed the

interview in her mind—a complete fiasco. She stood up. But seeing him walk toward her shifted her mindset. The closer he got, the wider the smile on his face grew.

"What?" she asked. "I was starting to wonder if I'd imagined our whole conversation, but your cup here gave me solace. Everything okay?"

"I had to call the folks at HR. The position has been filled."

Hannah sank into dismay, though he continued to smile happily.

"Oh. I see. Wow, okay." Her throat tightened, tears started to well up though she willed them not to. "I thought . . ."

"You got the job."

"It was—" She halted. "I what? What did you say?"

"You're hired. You got the job."

"But I thought—"

"I called to let them know I'd found the perfect candidate. But they wanted a full report on all the candidates—especially after I told them that we have some shared history from a couple decades ago—which is why it took me a while. They wanted to make sure I wasn't biased by that, but I told them we haven't seen each other since we were in our early twenties. But you're the one—you're clearly the one that deserves this position. You're the only one I talked to today who has the passion for bringing books to life. Everyone else just talked about what they could do or had done. Sorry for the wait. I didn't mean to leave you hanging."

"Oh my God," Hannah whispered. "Oh my God, I got the job. I got the job?"

Hannah threw her arms around him. Then immediately backed off and tried to pull herself together. Her restraint didn't hold more than a second before she hugged him again.

Before he let her go, he affirmed, "Congratulations!"

Hannah pulled back, straightening her sweater to regain her composure. The smile on her face and tears in her eyes betrayed the giddiness inside. She flapped her hands near her face, to stem the flow of tears, then put a fist to her mouth, gulping in a breath. She started to throw her arms around him again, trying to restrain herself, but he reached out to embrace her as she sputtered, "I—I can't—I—"

Holding Hannah lightened his heart in a way he hadn't felt for as long as he could remember. He'd found not only the right person for the job, but the person he'd been unconsciously seeking for a very long time.

CHAPTER 19

Taking Flight

HANNAH

"United flight 4399 to London will now begin boarding at Gate 47."

Hannah pulled out the crumpled itinerary, though she'd already checked it some twenty times. Yes, the flight numbers matched. She looked over her boarding pass to make sure she was at the right gate. She'd dozed off while waiting, clutching her carry-on to keep it safe during the long layover at JFK.

Exhausted, her mind reverted to old patterns—diving down rabbit holes of fearful thinking. *What if I get lost and end up in Germany? The only German I know is "ja." Saying yes to everything is dangerous and could lead to getting yelled at, accused of some inadvertent crime. Confession by confusion.* She took a long, deep breath to shake off the narrative. Her overactive imagination served well in writing, but not traveling. She forced herself to look at the destination listed at the gate and read it aloud: "London."

"Excuse me?" A young woman stood beside her, also watching the priority passengers board. "Sorry, I thought you said something to me," she said with a light British accent. Hannah shook her head. "Are you alright?"

"Yes. Of course."

"You have that look."

"What look?"

The young woman squinted. "Sorry, it's really none of my business."

Hannah was relieved to be in conversation with someone other than herself. "That's okay. What look?"

A smile spread over the woman's face. "I'm Gwen."

"Hannah." They awkwardly shifted their purses and carry-on luggage to manage a light handshake.

"Trepidatious."

"Fleet. Hannah Fleet."

Gwen laughed then reigned it in at the awkward look on Hannah's face. "Sorry, I meant how you look. My husband is always telling me I should stop using such big words, it's off-putting. I hope I didn't offend."

Hannah broke into a welcomed laugh. "Well, I thought it was an odd last name, but also didn't want to . . . you know . . . offend. I am a bit. Trepidatious, that is."

The next group for boarding was lining up. There seemed to be some holdup with a passenger at the front of the line. Hannah set her daypack on top of her small rolling suitcase.

Gwen smiled. "You have aerophobia? Sorry, I'm sure Mother would tell me that was a rude question. Flying used to make me dreadfully nervous. I'd be a wreck every time I had to fly."

"But you got over it?"

"Hypnotherapy. You looked rather like I used to feel."

"It's not so much the flying itself. It's everything else."

"Well, all good then." The line started to move, and passengers were now flowing past the gate attendant. Gwen and Hannah both checked their boarding passes to confirm again they were in the right group.

"Did you ever lose your luggage?" Hannah asked.

"Oh, God, don't get me started." A look of concern crossed Hannah's face. "It'll be fine, though. Really. Most of the time it arrives without a hitch."

The attendant picked up the mic. "Ladies and gentlemen, we

are now boarding group three."

"That's me," the young woman said and dashed to the back of the slow-moving line. Hannah allowed a few other passengers to get behind the young woman before she picked up her carry-on. Their group halted for a man in a wheelchair arriving late.

She used the opportunity to slow her breathing, the way Jaz had shown her. She tried to think of something happy, like the reconnection with James at Imprint Digital two weeks ago. What was this fear, really? Her baggage with clothes that didn't fit quite right or that she didn't even like anymore, garage sale jewelry, the cheap suitcase. Toothbrush with smashed bristles. So what if it was all lost? She could buy new things or live with what was left. That sounded appealing! A tad more expensive than not losing it—but manageable. She exhaled slowly. Calm flowed through her.

"We are now asking that all passengers for flight 4399 please board at this time. This is the *final call* for flight 4399." Hannah's eyes flew open. The line was gone and the woman with the microphone was staring at her. She hurried forward. At the end of the jetway, the last few passengers to board were hovering near the door. She touched the fuselage as she passed through the hatch, her private ritual. She added a smile of gratitude. The next time she touched the outside of the plane she'd be in London.

Hannah worked her way slowly down the aisle to her row. A large, gray-suited man filled the center seat. He looked uncomfortable—like it was his perpetual state—mouth in a well-established semi-grimace. She thought about the shift from her old version of normal—grateful to Jaz. And Maudie. And Allie. And James. The smile on her face grew as she forced her bag into the overhead compartment and pointed at the window. "That's my seat. May I?"

The man heaved himself up, pulling hard on the seat in front of him, whose occupant looked around in annoyance. Hannah smiled at her seatmate. "Thanks." He nodded. Fastening her seatbelt and confirming her seat back was in its upright position, she lifted the shade to watch the airport workers load baggage, then the guys with glow wands directing the pushback tractor.

A cloud bank cast a dark edge to the evening sky. A gradient of orange clung to the rim of distant streetlights that rested on the horizon. A plane landing on a cross runway set Hannah imagining who might be arriving in New York—until the accelerating roar and intensity of lift off gripped her.

What does it take for something to be considered real? Are my fears about flying less real than the plane itself? Are my dreams? Meditation and paying attention to her own breath—not just whether it smelled ok, but the sensation of it passing in and out certainly made her feel better. As did focusing on positive things. In her youth she didn't question the reality of her life—only *the point* of it. She now recognized things she used to consider obvious and fixed as matters of perspective and attention. She used to think life was an obstacle course of crap, but she was learning that gratitude could transform a disaster into an opportunity, pain into gain. Experience is personal, not universal—and reality subjective.

The lights below gave way to a deep black emptiness, and Hannah guessed they had circled over water before she saw city lights again. "Is that Brooklyn?"

Her seatmate leaned across her for a look. "Yep."

"Beautiful."

"From up here."

"A matter of perspective, I guess."

His face unraveled into a smile. "I guess it is."

As the plane climbed, the lights grew smaller and larger patterns of highways emerged. She felt graced with the changed perspective, thinking back to her first strained conversation with Jaz over ginger tea, and felt a resonant connection to the world below.

"Just imagine, there may be couples walking along in a park down there, holding hands and looking up at us and saying, 'I wonder where they're going tonight? Maybe there are people on that plane imagining us down here.'"

"Could be."

The wonder of it! *Time and space looping around like a stunt flyer, connecting us all through imagination. Or reality—whatever this is—but connecting us nonetheless whether we're fiction or non-fiction, poetry or science, music or dance. Awesome! Magnificent!*

Gray Suit seemed uncertain about whether to say anything further. *Perhaps he was trained as a young boy not to speak to strangers.*

"I'm fine," she said. He smiled again, nodded and closed his eyes. Hannah imagined: *him as a smart little boy, with straight black hair and wonder in his eyes, eager to discover the world, but reprimanded by a fierce, over-protective mother . . . until he stopped speaking to anyone.* Her mind rolled on to *his mom as a young woman who got too friendly with a man she met at a party who then raped her when she accepted a ride home. The rapist had been a child once, too—neglected in the space between his mother's alcoholism and his father's absence—who just needed to know that someone loved him. His mother, in turn, afraid of being alone, had turned to alcohol when her husband abandoned her. The husband found a woman who helped him rediscover laughter and peace . . .* On and on and on, circling back to her on this plane as a woman who had made two amazing friends, one who took her in as a stranger in need, and the other while delivering newspapers. Women who helped her wake up to how we are all one connected mass of humanity and consciousness. If the whole idea were not so invigorating, it would be exhausting because it was so . . . enormous.

Hannah felt the urge to write. She wrestled notebook and pen out of her daypack from under the seat. Random images drifted through her consciousness: pieces of a broken smoky-blue mug . . . a comforter with a green leaf pattern . . . lining kitchen drawers with contact paper . . . *Where do the random photos of the mind come from? Books? Films I've watched? Ads? Where do thoughts come from? Where do memories live?* She wandered in the mystery of everything.

As the plane carried her off into the dark, she began to write, lighter than she'd ever felt before.

CHAPTER 20

Clues & Views

Jim took a long drink from his water bottle, glad to be back in Marin County, hiking the hills of Big Rock Ridge on the northern side of Lucas Valley. The heat of the sun was comfortably offset by the cool breeze from the west. The Bay Area was starting to feel like home.

With his decision to stay put for awhile, he sensed he was on a journey of purpose and intention, unrelated to any location. People here discussed their journeys without blushing or backpedaling. He'd stopped thinking of the words "new age" and "weirdo" as even being related.

The ground beneath his feet was the same earth that supported the creature that was rustling dry live oak leaves nearby. He was surrounded by, connected to, life. Sparrows darted through air that buzzed with insects. They inhaled oxygen that had been exhaled by the oaks and bay trees as they breathed in the carbon dioxide he exhaled. *It's good to be alive.*

"What are you thinking about?" Hannah sat in the shade on a large rock, her long-sleeved shirt tied around her waist, daypack on the rock beside her, hair shining even in the shade.

"You know, I used to think life was me and about seven billion other separate, disconnected people moving through an objective—and, frankly, pretty harsh—'out there.' That connections had to be built out of nothing, worked at. That shit happens and we each just have to struggle through. Life was hard. Blows my mind how blind I was to how connected we are—just naturally, like connected to plants, to dirt even. Except right before a shower, of course!"

Hannah's laugh was a stream of water burbling around the roots of a thirsty tree. The ease with which it flowed and the love that flowed with it nourished Jim as it washed over him.

He continued, "I never used to even notice! And I'm not saying now I've figured it out and it's all magical and unicorns and fairy dust. It's not perfect. Or maybe it is somehow, and I just can't see it yet. But I don't feel powerless anymore."

Jim moved her pack aside and sat with her. "Tell me about Allison. Please."

Hannah nodded and looked out over the valley. "She's doing well. Engaged, but they haven't set a date. I told her we found each other. And that actually you hadn't left us, but that I took her away from you because I was scared. That you'd screwed up, yes, but that it wasn't that you'd abandoned us."

"I was such a wreck that day. Can you ever forgive me?"

"I have."

"Do you think she'll forgive me?"

"I think so. But she needs time. She's had a lifetime of believing a story that wasn't really true."

Jim smiled wryly. "Seems like a lot of us are doing that." The breeze in the dry rattlesnake grass that covered the hillside shushed their worries away. They sat quietly. "I'm glad you found her."

"Me too."

Jim got up and surveyed the valley below. Hannah squinted in his direction. "I want to ask you something . . . "

Jim's stomach braced. Then he remembered the sticky note on his mental mirror: "I create my own reality, and it's all good—even when it looks bad." He'd been posting various notes to help him shift his beliefs. From "life's a bitch—suck it up" to something more aligned with his new perspective. He squinted a questioning look at Hannah.

Having opened the door to this conversation, she might as well walk through it. "Does it seem . . . ? I mean, does it feel to you like . . . ? When we reconnected at the Expo . . . did you get the feeling . . . ?"

Jim laughed. "I'm not really sure until you finish one of those questions."

"Gah! I feel like I . . . I can't figure out what happened. It only makes some kind of sense if I let go of every idea I've ever had about what reality is. I'm not a New Agey, pendulum-swinging, Tarot-reading kind of person. Not that I reject that stuff completely, because I clearly don't have life all figured out. I used to think I did, but I definitely don't anymore. But I guess I'm just really wondering if you are as mystified as I am. Or if I am straight up delusional. Or crazy. Or—what the hell—prophetic or something. Do you know who killed Colonel Mustard?" She looked at him as if she had just asked something as simple as "Do you like peanut butter ice cream?"

Jim couldn't unravel the swirl of questions, but his heart danced faster as her monologue quickened, and time slowed to a halt in counterpoint to the wild emotional dance. The air between them filled with the energy of time holding its breath and slipped into his lungs like fog rolling in through the Golden Gate. It rolled back out with "Yes. And no."

Time held as still as Rodin's *Thinker*. Hannah blinked. A gopher poked its head out of a hole, looking at each in turn. Hannah blinked again. "Yes?" She set her chin on her hand, reminiscent of the sculpture, pondering the list of her questions that his "yes" might address. He rubbed his big toe with his other foot. The gopher retreated. Time released its breath into a gust of wind that flipped Hannah's hair into her face. She looked up at him.

"Maybe," he said slowly, as if rediscovering how to speak. "Maybe we're supposed to be together." The statement stretched between them like a living entity. In the absence of fear, the statement relaxed, drawing them closer as they wondered at it.

Hannah slipped off the rock. Jim moved towards her. The

statement softened further, pulling them with it. The space between them the size of a baby, they reached across it into an embrace rich with hope. Hannah relaxed into Jim as he pulled her close. His lips brushed her hair, her ear. He wanted to whisper something, to draw her inside, closer to his heart. The air felt more alive, all things more at peace, more possible than before she had reappeared in his life.

Words could only capture—not free—the feelings. So he held her silently.

Hannah released herself into his warm solidity, his scent. So right, so amazing the connection with him. Much as she loved words, silence spoke in this moment.

Jim took her face in his gentle hands, asking silently. Hannah nodded slightly. They kissed.

The gopher witnessed.

CHAPTER 21

Time Fold

Hannah stared at the water as they walked along the path that looked out over San Francisco Bay. "I used to have a terrible fear of drowning."

"Not anymore?" Jim asked.

"I don't think so."

"What changed?"

"I did. I used to be afraid of all kinds of things. A phobaholic."

"Like what?"

"Like flying. Even checking baggage."

"Seriously?"

"Yeah. Afraid they would lose my suitcase and my stuff."

"Not totally unreasonable."

"Except that my stuff was from Goodwill. Not much value."

"Except that it was yours."

"You don't have to justify my phobias, really. In my saner moments, I don't. Only in the throes of panic or fear can I seem to justify them. Oh, and laundromats in foreign countries."

Jim's laughed.

"You know, not understanding the currency—like how much to put in the machines. Walking through an alien land schlepping a bag of dirty underwear. The truth is out! You need to know I'm a bit crazy if we're going to . . . be together. You wouldn't want to discover this on vacation in Paris when you're out of underwear. Does my confession mean the end of our relationship?"

His arm around her shoulders, he turned her toward him.

"Hannah Fleet, I promise I will never ask you to do laundry in France. I can wash my own underwear—at home and abroad. Furthermore, I will protect you from the mysteries of foreign currencies and lost luggage for as long as we're together." Hannah smiled. "Which I hope will be a very long time."

Jim pressed his lips to hers.

"Picnic at the Marina?" he asked.

"You brought food?"

"I was never a Boy Scout, but my parents taught me that low blood sugar can lead to negative behaviors. I always carry food." He slipped his arm around Hannah's waist to feel the easy sway of her hips as they continued.

"If hunger causes negative behavior, I'd say my father was perpetually hungry. Starving. Ravenous."

"Sorry to hear that."

"It's okay. I only had to endure it for eighteen years."

Jim felt tension gather in her middle. Hannah sighed and the tension eased. He pulled her closer.

They passed other couples as they approached the Marina Green where kites were flying overhead, dogs romping. Hannah rested her head against Jim's shoulder. "Sorry. Didn't mean to go into Downsville." She smiled. "Maybe I'm just hungry."

"Got you covered. How about pecans? Tell me you like pecans."

"Love pecans."

"Score! Let's dig them out." Jim spread an old towel on the grass "a red carpet for the queen." With a magician's flourish, Jim pulled from the depths of his pack nuts and carrots, bread sticks and string cheese, cherry tomatoes, and a tub of hummus. As a finale he swept his arm to suggest that the blue sky, warm sunshine, cool bay breeze, and gorgeous view were all courtesy of Jim Wescott.

She sat with great decorum.

"Oh, and napkins." As he pulled out linen napkins, a harmonica dropped to the towel. "Oops, there's Marie."

Hannah looked up and around, but no one was approaching.

"Marie?"

"The harmonica. It was my mom's. I made her a deathbed promise to learn how to play—to try at least." He sat, rubbing his thumb along its side thoughtfully.

"Play something for me?"

He cradled the harmonica, closing his eyes as he played "Red River Valley."

"Beautiful."

"I'm still learning. Her dad played. I never got to hear him—died the year I was born. I carry it around so I'll practice."

They dipped carrots in the hummus, held them to salute, and crunched together. "Nice spread—I'm impressed. Do you always carry this much food?"

"Ahhh . . . no. You have found me out, my lady! I actually planned this."

Hannah shifted on the towel so they were back-to-back, leaning on each other. "We barely knew each other back then. We'd only been together a couple months before the accident. And then we had to figure out how to manage with a baby on the way."

"Yeah. I feel like we barely got to know each other."

"What was your family like? Happier than mine, I hope."

Jim chewed on his thoughts. "Functional. Happy, I guess. Mom was a teacher. That probably helped. Dad was my soccer coach for several years. We were pretty close. He had a good heart, except that it stopped working way too soon. I'm the only one left." Hannah leaned forward to turn to him. Jim stood, focusing on the calming water as it lapped against the boats, letting it ease the tightening in his heart.

"Didn't you have a brother?"

"Cal was killed a few years ago."

"Oh my God, I'm so sorry. I feel like I should've known that or did know it. Are you okay?"

"Getting there."

Hannah looked away, her eye catching something metallic

buried in the thick carpet of grass. "What's that?" A gust off the bay clinked hardware on masts, flicked a strand of her hair into her eyes.

"What's what?" Jim asked without shifting his gaze. The sailing vessels in the Marina floated and bobbed on waves rippling with light, adrift like Jim's thoughts.

"Something shiny. Sort of, anyway."

"Probably a bottle cap or gum wrapper."

"No, it's something else." She carefully pulled back the grass around the object. "It's a pocketknife."

Suddenly alert, he whipped around, staring at it. "That's mine," he said automatically.

Hannah smiled playfully. "Finders keepers." She pulled it out of the grass carefully, saw him fixated on the knife. "I was kidding, you know. You can have it if you want." Jim didn't move. "What is it?"

"That's the knife my dad gave me when I turned ten. I lost it the last time I lived here."

"What? That's crazy."

"I had cut myself and got upset and—I can barely remember anymore. But it's mine. That's so weird—to be right here, and you seeing it."

She handed it to him. Feeling dangerously close to something, Jim handed it back, trying to dismiss it, sensing it had sliced through some mysterious veil. "It's not even rusty. How can that be?"

Hannah felt uneasy, too close to some precipice. "Let's go."

Jim's breathing had changed. The air was dense, its salt more cutting. The edges of his vision blurred. The knife was all he could see. A tunnel formed around him—the darkness of forgetting something important. His mind gripped the knife, turned it over, examined it, ran memories carefully over its blade—*Cal eagerly watching me unwrap it on my birthday—whittling sticks for roasting hot dogs with Dad—cutting threads caught in a zip—*

"Are you okay?" Hannah's voice shook loose the darkness. He blinked, saw her sitting in the grass, eyes concerned, hand holding the knife. Her golden hair snatched the sun and shone. A gift of raw beauty. Who was this amazing woman? What web of the universe had brought them together in this moment? Who, in fact, was he? The questions shifted like ocean currents, blending into each other.

"Jim?" Hannah set the knife down beside her.

"I'm sorry," Jim said quietly. "I think I got lost there."

"You okay?"

"I think so. Not sure what happened. But I'm sure that's my knife." Hannah handed it to him again and he turned it over, "J.W." faintly visible on the handle. When he held it, a wave of loss washed over him, then retreated. He put it in his pocket. "Thanks." He looked away to compose himself.

The zephyr that had been caressing his cheeks eased him back to the present. His right hand fingered the knife in his pocket. Whatever loss it represented, he let it go as he emptied his lungs completely. *Now is all that matters.*

"Let's walk. You mind?" he asked.

"Sounds good."

He smiled. "I'm fine. That was a bit—I don't know—weird. Didn't mean to freak you out. Guess I was kind of freaked out myself. It was like I had lost something—not just the knife, but something really important. I'm not sure what. I couldn't really think at all, like I'd passed into some inaccessible zone. Sorry. Now I just sound crazy." He paused. "I'm not."

"It's okay. Really." Hannah slipped her hand into his and he received it gratefully. A soothing silence settled around them.

"You know, in the hospital after the accident, when the nurse told me I was pregnant—indirectly—if you hadn't overheard that, I'm not sure I would've told you. I probably would've just aborted while I had the chance. The Big Decision—it ripped me in two in ways I couldn't even articulate back then. Have the baby and give up everything—my writing, my dreams—just as I was getting started. Or erase the mistake with an abortion. It was *my* life—or hers—impossible. How could I choose only one?"

"I'm sorry," Jim said softly.

"You don't have to be. Don't be." She squeezed his hand.

"Maybe . . ."

"Maybe what?"

"Maybe we didn't."

"What do you mean?"

He was tentative, cautious. "Maybe both happened."

Hannah responded more with curiosity than criticism. "How?"

"I don't know. Just a feeling that there is more going on that what we can see or comprehend, more mystery than answers."

"You mean like parallel universes? Multiple versions of our lives?"

"I know it sounds crazy, but maybe."

Hannah squeezed his hand.

Jim returned the squeeze. "Does not knowing make you uneasy?"

"No. Not anymore. Seems like the less certain I am how the world works—or maybe I should say the more open I am to it— the more at peace I feel."

They turned left off Scott Street onto Beach. A beagle bounded around the corner at Avila and stopped with tail wagging at a fire hydrant. He looked at Jim briefly, cocked his head, then followed his nose to the scent-fest.

"That's Dog!" Jim said abruptly.

"You forgot your article." Hannah smiled.

"What article?" Jim watched Dog giving the hydrant a thorough sniff-down.

"In your sentence. If you're going to date a writer, you're going to have to make sure you don't leave unused articles lying around." Jim still looked confused. "That's *a* dog. Not 'that's dog'," she clarified.

"Oh! No. That's Dog. His name is Dog. I met him with a little girl—the same day I lost the knife." *What was the name of the cute kid who walked into my life and out again?* "Emmie. That was it—Emmie. Emmie and Dog."

They continued walking, silence walking in step with them.

Suddenly a little girl darted into Avila Street, followed by her mom with leash in hand. The girl wrapped her arms around Dog while mom attached the leash. She looked just the same as Jim remembered—same dress even, as if no time had intervened. It struck him as odd. Dog pulled her back up Avila toward the Marina, with mom close behind. Jim waved. They didn't notice. Just as well. He had no desire to revisit the awkwardness of that day.

Up ahead a man biked up Cervantes Boulevard toward the bay. "Maybe we could go biking together sometime," Jim said.

She looked at him, an image flashed across her mind of bike gears slipping. She nodded. "I'd like that."

Jim squeezed her hand. "I'd follow you anywhere."

"Follow?" The idea felt like a page turning.

"You can show me all your favorite places. Okay, I admit I'd love to watch your beautiful backside ahead of me wherever we go."

"Do you ever have déjà vu?"

"Absolutely. Did you ever see *Groundhog Day?* I used to have déjà vu all the time. I mean *all* the time."

"Are you now?" Hannah asked.

"Not really. Although there is something unsettling about this area. Every time I come to the Marina, I feel as if I've forgotten something, left something behind." Both thought of the knife. "Are *you* having déjà vu?"

"Maybe."

"Aren't we a pair!" They walked in silence for a bit.

At the intersection of Cervantes and Beach where they'd seen the man on the bike ride past, a woman turned left, pedaling her red bike hard toward them—harder than necessary for the level street. The rider glanced over. Their eyes met and locked in recognition. A sound like glass breaking startled Hannah as the woman with golden hair rode on.

THE BEGINNING

Gratitude

I am filled with gratitude.

For David Colin Carr, who helped me become a better writer in the process of editing. This book is so much better because of David. Thank you!

For Steve Napolitan, my mentor, who has been an amazing guide in my journey. Through his mentorship, my life has transformed in ways I'd yearned for but couldn't figure out how to manifest on my own. Thank you!

For my beta readers: John Byrne Barry, Ken Brown, Jerrilee Geist, Laurie Klein, Steve Napolitan, Jim Parker, Kathy Parker, Camilla Schneider, Lori Sommer, and Sue Staehli. Thank you for taking the time to read and provide valuable feedback that helped make this book better!

For my parents, who taught me to dream and follow my heart and believe in myself.

For my daughters, who have cheered me on all along the way. I love you beyond words!

For BAIPA (Bay Area Independent Publishers Association), where I learned most of what I now know about publishing.

For my ex-husband John, with whom I traveled a long way on this journey of discovery that life is so much more than I once perceived it to be. And even though we came to a point where it was better for us both to part ways, it was a road well-traveled when we were together.

For my team at Pro Audio Voices, who helped me bring my

own book to life in audio, including JS Arquin who partnered with me to narrate. You're the best!

And for my readers and listeners—the ones I wrote this for. Thank you for being part of my journey as well. I hope you will talk about it with friends, family, and others that you feel inspired to share it with. And with me! Please write a review and help spread the word. Thank you!

About the Author

Becky Parker Geist wanted to be an author since she learned what that meant, and her passion for stories has kept growing over the years. Her first book was written at age six in orange pencil on a very small notepad. Though not worthy of publication, she was nonetheless very proud of this accomplishment, and her parents were wonderfully encouraging (not like Hannah's).

After receiving her B.A. with a double major in Theatre and English, Becky went on to get her M.F.A. in Acting at University of Illinois, Champaign-Urbana. In 1981 she began narrating Talking Books for the Blind through the Library of Congress, narrating over seventy titles before moving with her husband and infant to California.

Becky co-founded two theatre companies in the San Francisco Bay Area: EDEN2 Theater Ensemble and Chaucer Theatre, which included an international tour as a performer. She has worked Off Broadway in NY (including Ars Nova Theatre, New York Theatre Workshop, and Signature Theatre) and the Bay Area (including A.C.T., the Mountain Play Association, and Marin Ballet) in a range of production roles.

Becky works with playwright Larry Klein as dramaturg and director. In 2022 her company produced a hybrid theatre-film production of *Colla Voce* in collaboration with Riverview Studios (her brother's company in New Jersey). In the film she performs the leading role. To view the film, visit bit.ly/collavoce. She always performs under the name Becky Parker.

Becky is the founder and CEO of Pro Audio Voices Inc., serving an international clientele with audiobook production—including full cast productions, Becky's favorite!—as well as marketing and podcasting services. Her intention is to inspire the world through the stories they bring to life. She believes that every time a great story comes alive, doors open—in the heart, in the mind, in the spirit. With each great story brought to life and each door that opens, positive change becomes possible, and the world changes—one story at a time.

Becky serves as President of BAIPA (Bay Area Independent Publishers Association) and presents frequently on the subject of audiobook production and marketing. She is also working closely with the team creating the Audiobook World Awards Academy.

The mother of three wonderful daughters who are also her best friends and colleagues, Becky lives in Portland, OR. In addition to writing, she also enjoys biking, hiking, dancing, playing the Native American flute, playing and inventing games—basically, all things creative.

Other books by Becky:
- *Audiobook Toolkit for Authors: Your Comprehensive Guide to Recording Your Own Audiobook*, available at authortoolkits.com
- *17 Tips on Selecting a Narrator for Your Audiobook: Insider's Guide to Choosing a Narrator You'll Be Thrilled With!*
- *Game Plan for Educators*
- *Rock-a-Bye Wiship*

For more info, visit *beckyparkergeist.com.*

DEAR READER,

If you enjoyed *The Left Turn*, I would appreciate it so much if you recommend it to a friend and/or write a review. There are hundreds of thousands of books published every year and it's a huge challenge to get the word out.

I would also love to hear from you. You can reach me at *becky@beckyparkergeist.com*.

Sneak Preview of Book 2
in the Split Universe Series

Hannah's heart pounded with anger, as if in its fury it was landing blows on Bob. How dare he! After all I've given up over the years to appease him! Rage and hurt and fear twisted together like a tornado in her gut, decimating the buildings of memories created together, wrenching up the life they'd shared by the roots that had grown out of her sacrifices. At the sight of an approaching tour bus, she had to fight the impulse to veer into its path.

She continued north on Cervantes Street, but tears blurred her vision. The towers of the Golden Gate Bridge smeared into a soft-edged swath against the blue sky. The world became a painter's palette of colors—a splotch of magenta blending into periwinkle into azure into yellow into red. An angry horn and shout from the yellow blot as she careened past the red octagonal smudge without slowing.

The cry of a newborn tore the air and Hannah turned left, following it.

A block up Beach Street, her vision cleared as she looked up into the eyes of a woman across the street—eyes she recognized, but didn't, her own, but not. Driven by the urgency of the infant's cries, she looked away and pedaled harder. A shattering crash of glass cut short the cries. Her breath caught as anxiety strengthened its grip. Hannah felt her own cry rising from deep inside as she raced toward the Marina. She needed a place to stop and wrestle with the anxiety that was now draining the colors around her to shades of gray, squeezing the life out of her.

The only sound that remained was the voice echoing in her head: What did I just do?

Made in the USA
Columbia, SC
18 August 2022